P9-DMR-267

THE MATCHSTICK CASTLE

THE MATCHSTICK CASTLE

Keir Graff

G. P. PUTNAM'S SONS

G. P. PUTNAM'S SONS
an imprint of Penguin Random House LLC
375 Hudson Street
New York, NY 10014

Library of Congress Cataloging-in-Publication Data is available upon request.

Printed in the United States of America.
9781101996225

1 3 5 7 9 10 8 6 4 2

Design by Ryan Thomann.
Text set in 11.5-point Maxime Pro.

For the real Cosmo

CHAPTER ONE

THE WORST SUMMER EVER

It was supposed to be the perfect summer. I was going to camp out, build forts, have adventures, and score the championship-winning goal in the New England All-Star Under-12 Soccer Tournament. When I wasn't doing those things, I was going to stay up late with my friends, eat as much junk food as I wanted, and pretty much do whatever I felt like until sixth grade started in September. It was going to be epic: the all-time, best summer *ever.*

Instead, I ended up in Boring, Illinois.

No, I'm not kidding. There's a town called Boring. And it is.

How did this happen?

I asked myself that question on the way to the airport in Boston, on the plane, and on the drive to Uncle Gary's house—which was actually just outside Boring, so I guess technically it was *almost* Boring—and was still asking myself that question early on the afternoon I arrived while Uncle Gary showed me how to use the educational software he had developed.

You guessed it: I was having summer school on a computer. Uncle Gary's program was called Summer's Cool, and if you think that's funny, don't laugh. You might be next.

"Now click here to start, Brian," said Uncle Gary, leaning over me and breathing stinky coffee breath into my airspace.

The screen in front of me showed subjects like language arts, math, science, social science, and art listed on a chalkboard in handwriting that was supposed to look like a little kid's. Why do grown-ups think all kids make their *R*s backward? And why would a kid be writing the lesson plan? That's the teacher's job, if you ask me.

Uncle Gary was pointing at *language arts*, so I clicked. A boy and girl scooted onto the screen. They looked like they were drawn by little kids, too—I'm not very good at drawing, but I could have done a better job. I was starting to feel like I was in kindergarten.

"*I'm Darren!*" said the boy, in an annoying little-kid voice.

"*And I'm Dara!*" said the girl, in the same voice, only higher pitched.

"*You picked language arts!*" they said together, sounding twice as annoying. "*Ready . . . get set . . . learn!*"

The chalkboard disappeared, and a story opened like the pages of a book.

"After you read the story, there will be a quiz," said Uncle Gary. "If you get enough answers right, it will let you move on to the next lesson. If you get too many wrong, you'll be prompted to reread the passages that caused you difficulty."

"You really made this?" I asked.

"Well, I did have a little assistance from some *highly* respected educational engineers," said Uncle Gary proudly.

I should have mentioned that my cousin, Nora, was sitting about three feet away on the other side of a folding table in the middle of Uncle Gary's office. She obviously didn't need any help. She had her headphones on and was clicking away like she was getting paid a penny per click. She's one year older than me and about two inches taller. Uncle Gary had spent most of the ride from the airport telling me what an amazing student she was. According to him, she was the smartest girl in her class, the smartest girl in her school, maybe even the smartest girl in the whole country.

And who knows? Maybe he was right. I hadn't seen Nora since I was five years old and I slimed her with a booger at somebody's wedding. I figured she'd just try to get me back—hadn't she ever played booger tag?—but she started crying and I had to go sit in the car.

I'm not exactly a good student. But I'm great at soccer, and climbing, and . . . well, lots of things.

So far, Nora and I weren't hitting it off any better than last time. When Uncle Gary brought me from the airport, she looked at me like I was a birthday present she'd gotten three years in a row. And, in the couple of hours since then, she'd been acting like she wished she could return me to the store.

"Think you've got the hang of it, Brian?" asked Uncle Gary.

Nora stopped clicking and looked up, like she was curious how I would answer. She reminded me of a scientist studying a chimpanzee.

"Sure," I said. It didn't look that hard, even for me.

"Great. Then I pronounce Summer's Cool officially in session!"

While I put on my headphones, Uncle Gary crossed the room, sat down at his desk in the corner, and started working on a computer with two big screens. He was the kind of guy who was hard to describe because there wasn't really anything you remembered about him—he didn't have glasses, or a mustache, or even very much hair on top of his head. If he got kidnapped and the police asked me what he was wearing, I wouldn't have had a clue.

His office was the same way. It reminded me of the big office-supply store I went to with my dad a few months ago when he needed to buy some new report covers for the deep-space data he'd printed out. The store had all these fake offices set up that made me think of grown-ups playing work the way some kids played house. All Uncle Gary's office was missing was the price tags.

The only thing that made it interesting at all was the old-fashioned model ships on top of the bookshelves. I especially liked a fast-looking one with a red smokestack. I wanted a closer look, but they were all out of reach.

Which I'm sure was the point.

If I could, I would have climbed aboard that ship, raised a skull-and-crossbones flag, and steamed right out of Boring, Illinois, forever.

Four days ago, I was walking home from the last day of school, kicking my soccer ball down the sidewalk past the other row houses and making plans for the summer. But when I got home, everything changed in a nanosecond.

My dad was running around the house, trying to do three things at once. While I followed him upstairs to his bedroom, he told me he'd gotten a phone call that morning from the National Science Foundation. If he could be ready by Monday, they said, he could go to the South Pole. He's an astronomer, and one of the most powerful telescopes in the world is at the South Pole. He'd been applying to go for so many years that none of us thought it would actually happen.

As he lugged his suitcase back downstairs, he explained that the astronomer who was posted there slipped on the ice and broke her right hand and her left arm. How do you slip on the ice in Antarctica? Don't they give you spikes or something for your boots? And it's not like you don't know you're on a continent completely covered in ice. But the deal was that my dad would fly down on the plane that would bring the other astronomer back.

"This is a once-in-a-lifetime opportunity," he said, opening his suitcase on the kitchen table and then picking up his phone, which was beeping like it was about to blow up. "I couldn't say no."

My brothers had to be excited, too. Barry, who's cool but goes to college, already had plans to spend the summer in Maine getting certified as a wilderness guide. And Brad—he's annoying but still lives with us because he's in high school—would be peeing his pants because he was going to get to spend his summer working in a pizza parlor and playing video games with his best friend, Isaac. Dad had already talked to Isaac's parents and they'd invited Brad to stay with them.

"Everyone else is getting to do something awesome," I said. "What about me?"

Dad looked up from his phone and gave me a here's-the-bad-news smile.

"You're just as important as everyone else, Brian, but most people already have plans for the summer," he said.

"I could stay with Uncle Sean," I suggested.

If I couldn't stay home, Uncle Sean was definitely my first choice. He was always doing something exciting.

"He's going to be taking photographs in Mongolia," said my dad.

"How about Grammy and Grampop?"

Summer at their house wouldn't be exciting, exactly, but their guest room had a TV, their fridge was stocked with soda, and there was an overgrown, abandoned factory I wanted to explore just down the road.

"They're heading out west to a seniors-only RV roundup. No kids allowed, I'm afraid."

"How about Oscar? Or Diego?"

They were my best friends and my teammates on the Boston Beans, which is the top under-12 soccer team in Eastern Massachusetts.

Dad shook his head. "Oscar's family is taking a Caribbean cruise, and Diego already shares his room with his grandma. But at your age, I'd rather have you stay with family, anyway. I'm sure your mother, if she were here, would agree."

I had no way of knowing what she would or wouldn't have wanted. I never knew my mom—she died when I was really little. My dad talked about her a lot, and there were lots of pictures of her around the house, but he only brought her into an argument when he really wanted to win it. I was doomed.

"Then where?" I asked, slumping into a chair.

"Your uncle Gary and aunt Jenny said they'd host you for the summer."

Of all the places I could have been sentenced to spend the summer—including a desert, jail, the moon, and outer space—my absolute last pick would have been Uncle Gary's house in

Boring, Illinois. It's not often a town is so perfectly named for its residents. But Uncle Gary, Aunt Jenny, and Cousin Nora were the most boring people I had ever met. I had never once heard of them doing anything remotely interesting.

"Think of it as an adventure," said my dad, tapping his phone with his thumbs.

"That's easy for you to say. You're *actually* going on an adventure."

Dad put his phone in his suitcase—where I knew he'd forget it—came around behind me, and gave my shoulders a rub. "You never know, Brian. You might have one, too."

If he could see me now, I thought. On the computer in front of me, Darren and Dara were waving their arms like they were trying to get my attention. Their voices came through my headphones: "*We're waiting! Are you ready to start?*"

Uncle Gary looked up. I guess he noticed that Nora was the only one clicking.

"Is there a problem, Brian?" he asked in that tone people use when they already think there is a problem, and the problem is you.

I took off my headphones. "It's just that my dad never said anything about summer school. I wouldn't have to do this if I was at home."

"Studies show that, over long summer vacations, most kids forget a large portion of what they learned during the previous year, Brian. They take two steps forward and one step back."

Uncle Gary spoke slowly, like he wasn't sure I would understand. He even illustrated the two steps forward and one step back with his hand, like his fingers were little legs walking. I wondered if my dad had told him I was bad at school.

"That's why I created the Summer's Cool software," he continued. "You and Nora are my beta testers. And you're the first ones to benefit."

Nora, of course, had stopped clicking and was watching me again. I swear I still hadn't seen her blink. You'd think her eyeballs would dry out.

"Did my dad say I have to do this?"

"He agreed that you would abide by my rules while living in my house."

"But . . . he didn't say I had to do this *specifically*?"

"These plans all came together very quickly, as you know. We didn't have time to discuss *every* detail."

"I want to ask him. If he never had me do summer school before, I don't know why he would suddenly want me to start doing it now."

Uncle Gary's face tightened, like a smile and a frown were at war beneath the surface.

"Fine," he said. "Ask your father. But until he replies, we'll do things my way. Deal?"

"Okay," I said.

For now, I thought.

Uncle Gary turned back to his own computer.

Nora was still staring at me. I gave her my best what-are-YOU-looking-at face, but she didn't blink. So I tried my zombie face instead: I opened my mouth so far it looked like my jaw was broken and rolled my eyes back until I could practically see my own brain. She stared at me for a few more seconds and then calmly went back to work.

What a freak!

I put the headphones on again.

"*We're waiting!*" chorused the kids on the computer. "*Are you ready to start?*"

I hit pause, and mute, then opened a new browser window and signed on to my e-mail. I knew my dad was still on his way to Antarctica, but I wanted my message to be waiting for him when he got there.

Dear Dad,

So far, this is the worst summer ever. Nora still hates me, and even worse, Uncle Gary is using us as human guinea pigs for this dumb software he made called Summer's Cool. I told him you would say I don't have to do any kind of summer school, so please tell him as soon as you can. And also tell him it's okay for me to stay up late, to have soda with caffeine in it, and to use my spending money on whatever I want. If Grammy and Grampop drive through Illinois, they should pick me up. I would rather hide in the back of their RV all summer then stay here. HELP ME!

Love, Brian

PS I hope Antarctica is cool. Send pictures of penguins.

"It's spelled *t-h-a-n*, Brian," said Uncle Gary.

I jumped, thinking he had sneaked up behind me. But he was still at his desk, eyes glued to his monitor. Was he using spyware to look at my screen?

PPS This is private, Uncle Gary! I typed.

"While you're in the school environment, I have the right to monitor your computer," he answered in his I'm-speaking-slowly-so-you'll-understand voice. "You can always save personal messages for after school."

"Well, thanks for telling me."

"Now you know."

After deleting the last line, I clicked send, waited anxiously while the computer screen seemed to freeze, and then swallowed in relief when I saw that the message had been sent.

"And now it's time to get to work," said Uncle Gary.

I un-paused and un-muted Summer's Cool.

"*Welcome back!*" said Darren and Dara. "*Are you ready to learn?*"

CHAPTER TWO

INTO THE WOODS

When Aunt Jenny came in with a tray that had a mug of coffee and a cookie for Uncle Gary, I guessed it was quitting time. Aunt Jenny worked from home, too, making craft projects that she sold online. I don't know who buys dolls with yarn hair or little signs that say *Bless This Mess*, but I guess it's a better job than developing software that has the potential to ruin the summer of every kid in America. Uncle Gary checked his watch and picked up a big brass bell with a wooden handle.

"School's over for today," he said, ringing the bell like he was trying to break it in half. "We'll get a full day in tomorrow, starting at eight thirty."

It seemed to me that he could have just said the words without ringing the bell. The bell was so loud I practically had to read his lips.

I couldn't get out of the room fast enough. The whole thing was weird. At my house, people eat when they're hungry and do homework when they have to and usually sleep in until the very last minute. There are no bells and nobody brings anyone a snack on a tray. It's a lot more frantic in some ways but a lot more relaxed, too. Honestly, I couldn't see how my dad and Uncle Gary were even related.

"Enjoy your free time!" said Aunt Jenny. She was a short, heavy lady with spiky hair and bright red glasses. Maybe she was trying to make up for her husband looking so uninteresting.

"Do you like soccer?" I asked Nora as we went into the hallway.

"What do you think?" she asked me back.

"Well, I don't know. That's why I'm asking."

It's so annoying when people answer a question with another question.

"Not particularly," Nora said.

"Well, want to give it a try? I brought my ball—we could play in the backyard."

Nora gave me a look that said she was sorry I was so stupid, but it obviously wasn't her fault. "I don't have time for things like sports."

She went into her room and closed the door. What was wrong with her? All I did was invite her to kick a ball around, and she was acting like I asked her to smell my farts.

Well, Brian, I said to myself. *It looks like you're a team of one.*

. . .

The backyard was huge, I realized once I got out to the patio. It was also empty except for two tiny trees and a big wooden shed. The lawn was as short as a putting green, but there weren't any bushes or flowers and the patio chairs were all pushed in under the table. Uncle Gary, Aunt Jenny, and Nora didn't get out much.

The backyards on either side of Uncle Gary's looked basically the same, and the backyards on the other side of those did, too. They were all separated by chain-link fences. But behind all the yards was a long, tall mound made of dirt and rocks and tree roots. It made me feel like we were in one of those trenches they dug back when they were fighting World War I. On the other side of it was a forest.

I put my ball down on the grass. Boy, was it hot. Even my hair felt hot. I dribbled back and forth across the yard a few times, cutting left and spinning right like I was moving through a crowd of defenders, but after only a few minutes, I felt sweaty and bored. Playing alone just wasn't the same as playing with friends.

I decided to practice shooting, kicking the ball with the laces of my shoes so it rocketed past the arms of the helpless goalkeeper. I imagined that one section of the fence was the goal and shot at it, hitting it square and making the chain links rattle. I picked up the ball and did it again, this time trying to hit the corner of the goal, where it would be harder for the keeper to reach. The trick was to keep my weight over the ball. If I leaned back, the ball would go up and . . .

I watched as the ball flew over the fence. It hit the mound of dirt, bounced over the top, and disappeared down the other side.

Good thing nobody was watching. I crossed the yard, climbed the fence, and scrambled up the dirt until I stood at the top. My ball was caught in a bush. I slid down and got it, then crouched in the shade at the edge of the dark, leafy woods. There was a cool breeze that felt good on my sweaty skin. The trees grew close together, but I saw a narrow path winding between them.

At last! Something that doesn't look boring. Tucking my ball under my arm, I decided to see where it went.

The forests I was used to were more like parks, with lots of room around the trees. But this forest was crowded. It had so many bushes and branches and tangles and snarls that it would have been impossible to move without the path.

Unfortunately, the path wasn't a very good one, and it was hard to tell what it was for or where it was going. It zigged and zagged and curved and hooked. Before long, I was so turned around that I didn't know if I was heading for the heart of the forest or about to reach the backyard again.

Maybe there wasn't anything interesting here after all. I decided to turn back. But now the path behind me didn't look like a path at all. And the way ahead didn't look very clear, either. Where the heck was I?

A beetle as big as a raisin was crawling up my arm. *Gross.* I squished it and wiped it off on a leaf. Then a cloud of gnats swarmed me and, before I knew it, one of them got in my mouth. I spit it out, then spit two more times for good measure. Bugs were a major downside to exploring. Unless, of course, you were exploring Antarctica—which may sound like it's named after ants but isn't.

I wasn't exactly panicking, but at the same time, I knew I was lost. I was a city kid. To me, no two street corners looked alike, but every tree looked pretty much the same. And there were a lot more trees than street corners.

Still definitely not panicking, I started running, but the farther I went, the darker and quieter the woods got.

I stopped, panting, my heart beating like a bucket drum.

Then I heard a man's voice—there was someone else in the woods. I opened my mouth and was about to yell for help, but something made me stop. Part of it was the way the person was talking: quietly, like he didn't want to be heard.

And part of it was what he said: "You go around to the right, and I'll go around to the left."

He was with someone. And they were trying to sneak up on someone.

Me?

I didn't move a muscle, except for my heart and lungs,

which I couldn't stop, no matter how much I wanted to. I searched the forest but saw nothing.

It was almost perfectly silent.

Then a twig snapped.

Then I heard the crack of a gun—a big gun. It sounded like a sonic boom in a barrel.

At home, they teach us to throw ourselves on the ground if we hear gunfire. No one needed to tell me here. While the sound was still echoing through the trees, I was facedown in the mud trying to make myself as flat as a forest pancake.

There was another gunshot, and the two voices shouted, or maybe there were three.

Then I heard something else. Actually, I felt it first, a rumbling in the ground like an approaching train. Something was crashing through the bushes. It was snorting and grunting and its feet were pounding the earth, coming closer.

I lifted my head at the exact same moment it exploded out of the bushes—and jumped right at me.

CHAPTER THREE

OFF-LIMITS

I got a glimpse of tusks, hooves, and stiff gray fur as whatever it was flew over me and thundered into the trees. I heard bushes ripping and bark chipping, like it was turning the forest into salad.

What *was* that? It looked like a pig crossed with a goblin. Fortunately, it hadn't stopped to stab and eat me. I guessed it was running away from the men who were hunting it.

I heard more shouting, but the voices were getting farther away. I wanted to get up and shout back, to ask for help and directions, but I was shaking so much I could hardly move. And if you think that makes me a chicken, why don't you lie in the mud and let a goblin-pig come crashing at you?

By the time I calmed down enough to stand up and yell, the forest was silent again.

"Hello?" I shouted. "Anybody out there? HELLO!"

Nobody answered.

I turned around slowly, looking for the path, but I couldn't see where I had come from. The woods around me were as blank as a wall.

Actually, that wasn't totally true. I could see where the animal's hooves had left prints in the mud, coming and going. It had broken branches on some bushes, too. I could even see deep scratches on a tree where its tusks had scraped the bark. That gave me an idea: If I looked carefully, could I find my tracks?

To my right, a tall piece of grass was bent in half. Below the grass, a shoe—the same length as mine—had squished a leaf into the mud. The heel of my shoe had to point toward Uncle Gary's, right?

I picked up my ball and started following the trail. It wasn't easy. Where the ground was dry, there weren't any footprints and I had to look extra hard for clues. A couple of times I even had to guess, but by that time I was mostly sure what direction I needed to be going.

I was pretty proud of myself. While I walked, I could almost imagine I was an explorer on an adventure. I hardly noticed the bugs that swarmed around me and got stuck in my hair. And, when I climbed the big pile of dirt behind Uncle Gary's house, I actually felt happy to see it.

Well, almost happy.

Nora was outside, working at the patio table in the shade of a big umbrella. The way she stared at me while I climbed the fence, you'd think I was Bigfoot. I couldn't wait to tell her what happened.

"You're never going to believe what just happened!" I said as I crossed the yard.

"Let me guess: You took last place in a mud-pie-eating contest?"

"Ha-ha, very funny. I went into the woods to get my soccer ball, and followed a path, and got lost, and heard gunshots, so I hit the deck, and then this crazy-looking goblin-pig animal jumped out at me, but fortunately it went over me and kept running."

Nora stared at me, her pen hovering over a page in a green notebook. If she ever entered a staring contest, I'd bet a year's allowance that she'd win.

Then she said, "You went into the woods?"

I threw up my hands. "Yes. That's where this whole thing happened. Have you even been listening?"

"We're not supposed to go into the woods."

"Well, nobody told me. Aren't you even a little bit interested in the goblin-pig?"

She put her pen in the notebook and closed it, marking her place. She frowned, like she was thinking, but you'd think she would have smiled if she liked thinking so much. "Are you sure it wasn't a regular pig?"

"Yes, I'm sure," I said, taking a step toward the house. "Regular pigs don't have fur and giant fangs. And besides, who would hunt a regular pig with a gun?"

"The weirdos who live in the woods, that's who."

I shook my head, disgusted. "You're missing the point of this story."

"Well, I wouldn't tell Dad if I were you," said Nora.

I waited to see if she'd blink, but of course she didn't, so I went inside. Uncle Gary and Aunt Jenny were in the kitchen cooking dinner.

"What happened to your clothes?" asked Aunt Jenny, her eyes widening as she looked up from the pot she was stirring.

"I was exploring the woods," I said proudly.

Uncle Gary put down the knife he was using to cut broccoli. "You went into the woods?"

"Yeah. I just thought I'd take a look, but then I went a little farther than I planned, and then I got lost, and *then*—"

I was just realizing that Nora was right, and I shouldn't tell him about the goblin-pig, when he interrupted me and saved me the trouble of making up a different story.

"You are not allowed to go into the woods, Brian," he said sternly. "They're off-limits."

Aunt Jenny put a hand on his arm. "Gary, he didn't know."

"Why are they off-limits?" I asked.

"The land beyond that big berm of dirt isn't part of Boring," said Uncle Gary. "Once you enter the woods, you're trespassing on private property."

"Who owns it?"

"A very unusual family," answered Aunt Jenny, making

the word *unusual* sound like a code word for *crazy people you wouldn't ever want to mess with unless you're crazy, too.* "We see them in town once in a while, but mostly they keep to themselves."

"If you run into them, keep your distance," said Uncle Gary.

"It's hard to believe anybody owns that land," I said. "It looks wild."

"Because they don't maintain it!" said Uncle Gary angrily. "It's like we're living in the subdivision at the edge of civilization. For all we know, there are dangerous wild animals in that forest!"

Well, that part was true. I was glad Nora warned me. That was actually nice of her. If they knew I'd almost gotten run over by some crazy animal with hooves and tusks, they'd probably lock me in the basement. And I didn't want to say or do anything that would make it harder to go back into the woods because, even if they were filled with hunters and wild animals, they were the only thing that kept Boring from completely living up to its name.

"So who is this family?" I asked. "What are they like? Do they have any kids?"

"How did you get so *dirty*, Brian?" asked Aunt Jenny, conveniently changing the subject.

"Making mud pies?" I shrugged and grinned. If they weren't going to give straight answers, I wasn't, either.

Aunt Jenny shook her head. "Hurry downstairs and get cleaned up before dinner."

I gave up and went down to my room. Did I mention that I had to sleep in the basement? Uncle Gary's office took up what should have been the guest bedroom, so I was in the cold, concrete storage area downstairs. Half the room was full of plastic shelves stacked with plastic boxes containing things like WINTER CLOTHES and TAX RETURNS. I had a little folding bed and a small dresser and a reading lamp, but that was about it. The tiny, high window made it feel like a prison cell.

There was a bathroom next door that looked like Uncle Gary had started to build it and then quit halfway. Electrical cords and pipes snaked through two-by-fours in an unfinished wall. A toilet sat on bare concrete, the sink rested in a plywood cutout, and the dusty shower stall looked like it had never been used, if the spiderwebs filling its corners were anything to go by.

I wondered how long I could go without showering before Aunt Jenny smelled what I was up to.

I took off my dirty clothes and dropped them in the corner, then put on clean jeans and a T-shirt. In the bathroom, a hairy spider was trying to climb out of the sink. It was so big it looked like it could eat Cheerios. I poured water on it until it lost its grip and slipped down the drain, then pulled the stopper before I washed my face and hands.

Dinner at my uncle's house couldn't have been more different from dinner at home. For starters, Uncle Gary had Nora and me set the table with knives, forks, and spoons, place mats, and cloth napkins. Then, at six o'clock on the dot, everyone sat down to eat together. The food wasn't fancy or anything—baked chicken, rice, and broccoli, with milk for the kids and iced tea for the grown-ups—but everyone took everything so seriously that it reminded me of report card day at home, the only day of the year when my brothers and I ate quietly and said *please* and *thank you*, hoping to distract our dad from the inevitable.

"And how was your day?" Uncle Gary asked Aunt Jenny.

"Fine, dear, how was yours?" said Aunt Jenny.

This seemed weird to me because Uncle Gary and Aunt Jenny both worked at home. Shouldn't they both be pretty up to date on that topic?

But apparently they had both run errands before picking me up at the airport, so they did have something to talk about. Aunt Jenny told Uncle Gary about her amazing trip to the grocery store, and Uncle Gary told her about his thrilling trip to city hall to renew his driver's license, while I wished I could talk about the goblin-pig and wondered if my dad would see any polar bears in Antarctica. Did they have polar bears there?

I ate the chicken and rice but avoided the broccoli. We never had broccoli at home. Dad didn't like it, either.

"Eat your broccoli, Brian," said Uncle Gary. "No broccoli, no ice cream for dessert."

I felt like I was four years old, but I ate the broccoli anyway. I really like ice cream.

But I should have guessed they'd only have vanilla.

Uncle Gary and Aunt Jenny never did get around to asking me about my day, which was probably a good thing. If they had asked, they would have gotten an earful.

After dinner, Uncle Gary announced that he was going to his office to "model," which made me think of a fashion model posing for the camera, but apparently meant making little ships out of wood and string. Aunt Jenny said she had crafting to do and headed for her workshop downstairs. Which left Nora and me to clear the table and wash the dishes.

Why do people use so many plates and pieces of silverware when they know they're going to have to clean them? At home, we used our fingers to eat pizza and plastic forks to eat Chinese food, with paper towels or paper plates we could just throw away.

Nora made me wash while she dried, which was the wrong order because she kept handing things back to me and telling me to wash them again. I admit I'm not very good at washing dishes, but I could have done just fine with the towel if she'd let me.

Finally, we were done, and Nora disappeared upstairs to her room. I didn't really know what to do, so I went into the living room to watch TV. At least they got the same shows in Illinois, even if they were all on at the wrong times.

After a while, I had to go to the bathroom. The upstairs bathrooms had to be nicer than the one in the basement, right? I left the living room and went into the tall entryway, then climbed a short flight of stairs. Suddenly, the house felt smaller: As I walked down a dark hall, the doors were all crowded together. The first one I came to wasn't closed all the way, so I opened it and looked in.

Inside was a room, two or three times bigger than my room at home, with a bed and a closet and a beanbag chair and a long window that looked out on the forest behind the house.

In the twilight, the trees looked spooky but cool. The dead ones that didn't have any leaves looked like giant skeleton hands reaching out of the ground. I wanted a closer look, so I took a few steps forward, then stopped when I realized Nora was sitting at a desk against the wall to my right. She was hunched over with her back to me, writing under a small desk lamp.

I tried to back up and leave without her noticing, but I bumped the door with my elbow. It made a hollow *DOONG* sound, and my arm got that tingling feeling that meant I'd hit my funny bone.

Nora jumped and spun around, shutting her green notebook and holding it against her stomach.

"What are you doing in my room?" she asked suspiciously.

I rubbed my arm. Funny bones are no joke. "I was looking for the bathroom."

"Does my chair look like a toilet? Does the bed look like a bathtub?"

"Come on, Nora—"

"You were spying, weren't you?"

"Spying? I just need to go to the bathroom!"

Nora rolled her eyes like I was making up a crazy story. "This room—and everything in it—is private, and it stays private, do you understand?"

"*Fine,*" I said.

"You'll find the bathroom two doors down on the other side of the hall," said Nora, advancing toward me. "Or you can use the one *downstairs* by *your room*."

I started backing up. "Is it all right if I relocate the spiders to your bathroom?"

Nora stared at me until I was out of sight. Even though her constant staring was getting on my nerves, I thought maybe I should buy her some eyedrops or something. If left untreated, she might end up with a bad case of lizard eyes.

I headed down the hall. I had something important in common with Nora: She didn't want me there, and I really, really didn't want to be there, either.

But why was her homework such a big secret?

Uncle Gary made us brush our teeth at eight thirty and turn off the lights by nine o'clock. It took me a long time to fall asleep. Only a few days ago, everything in my life was perfectly normal. Tonight, I was lying in a strange bed, wondering how people who were related to each other could be so different. I had started the summer thinking my biggest challenge would be trying to win a soccer tournament, but now I wouldn't even get to play. That didn't seem like such a big deal anymore. Now my biggest challenge would be surviving the summer—without going crazy.

CHAPTER FOUR

LOST IN THE WOODS . . . AGAIN

Dad didn't answer my e-mail that day, or the day after that, so I wrote another one on Wednesday, and this time I used capital letters and exclamation points. I told him he'd made a terrible mistake sending me to Illinois and that Uncle Gary was cruel—well, maybe not cruel exactly, but, well, staying inside all day doing homework in June was a kind of torture, so *YES,* I wrote on the last line, *HE IS BEING CRUEL!*

But Dad didn't write back. I hoped everything was all right. I had arrived in Boring on Monday, and I knew he wouldn't even have landed at the Amundsen-Scott South Pole Station until Tuesday night at the earliest. And since the South Pole uses the same time zone as New Zealand, which is seventeen hours ahead of Illinois, any message I sent today wouldn't reach him until tomorrow. But didn't that mean his answers should have arrived yesterday?

Story problems always gave me trouble, whether they were in school or real life. I was sure Nora could have helped me out, but *could have* isn't exactly the same thing as *would have*.

Meanwhile, summer school continued. If Uncle Gary liked teaching so much, why didn't he do it in a school, with actual students? In his house, he announced the start of the "school day," and every period in it, by ringing his bell. I hated that stupid bell.

"Class" started at eight thirty, "recess" was at ten fifteen, and lunch was at noon. After lunch, we were allowed forty-five minutes of free time, which I used to practice soccer, even though it was so hot out that it felt like I was practicing in a sauna. And then, at one thirty, we had to go back to the "classroom" for the final two hours and fifteen minutes of the day. One time, I came back from free time five minutes late, and Uncle Gary said I would have to do an extra half hour of lessons at the end of the day.

But when I complained, Uncle Gary told me that I should be proud to be part of what he called his "bold experiment."

"You see, Brian, it's now possible for kids to learn everything they need to know about the world right here, on a screen." He tapped my laptop. "It's the optimal learning environment, perfectly safe, where the teacher has one hundred percent awareness of—and control over—the curriculum."

"I hate to break it to you, but we already use apps in school."

"This software is different," insisted Uncle Gary. "Because it has been optimized for my own super scholar, Nora."

Nora's whole body clenched. "*Dad,*" she groaned.

"Parents who enroll their kids in my summer-learning program will send their kids back to school even smarter than they left it. And who knows? Maybe someday you'll have Summer's Cool all year round."

From the dreamy look on Uncle Gary's face, I think he honestly thought that was a good idea.

I probably shouldn't have laughed.

"What's so funny, Brian?"

"I was just thinking about having Darren and Dara teach kids for eight years in a row. They'd probably all end up"—I imitated their high pitched monotone—"*talking the same way!*"

"Don't make fun of Darren and Dara," scowled Uncle Gary.

I think I actually hurt his feelings. But he started it.

At lunch on Friday, Nora was writing in her green notebook while I rolled my ball back and forth under the table with my feet and wished my carrot sticks would eat themselves. I wondered why my cousin was the way she was. If I was an only child, I would have been happy to have someone my age around. Maybe she was so used to spending all her time with adults that she had forgotten how to be a kid.

"Could you please stop kicking that ball?" asked Nora without looking up. "I'm trying to concentrate."

I stopped. Nora didn't say thank you.

I decided to give her another try. "Want to go outside and play soccer? I know you said you don't play, but I could teach you. I bet you'd be great at it."

That last part sounded funny even to me, but I was desperate. Nora just kept writing, bent over the table, her pencil scratching across the blue-lined paper.

"I know you heard me, Nora."

She nodded her head.

"But you don't want to play."

She shook her head. I sighed so hard that wisps of Nora's hair fluttered in the breeze.

I started tapping the ball back and forth again. I couldn't help it—sometimes my feet had a mind of their own. "Why do you like school so much?" I asked.

Finally, she looked up.

"Is that what you think? That I like school?"

"You work really hard, even when you don't have to, and you never complain. So yeah, I'd say you like it."

"Do you like brushing your teeth?"

"Nobody likes brushing their teeth, not even dentists," I said.

"But you do it, right?"

"Well, duh."

"Because you don't want to get cavities."

I saw where she was going with this. Pushing my chair back, I stood up and started dribbling my ball around the table. "But you don't have to brush your teeth all day long."

Nora put down her pencil and sighed. "School doesn't last forever. And you're not supposed to do that in here."

"I guess you're really looking forward to being an adult and getting a job," I said, ignoring her.

"Some of us are planning to grow up, you know. You can't be a kid forever."

I felt like she was saying that I was too dumb to understand what she was talking about. And that made me mad.

I stopped my ball with my foot and looked at Nora's notebook, at her fancy squiggly handwriting—she wrote in cursive that, upside down, I couldn't read any better than Chinese.

"I mean, you're always doing homework in your precious green notebook. It's actually kind of sad. Because you're a teacher's pet, and your dad's the teacher!"

Nora's cheeks turned red as she fixed me with a death glare.

"What makes you think I'm doing homework?"

"If it's not homework, then what is it?"

"None of your business."

She started writing again.

My head felt hot, like I was hanging upside down on the monkey bars. Without thinking, I reached out and snatched the notebook from her.

Nora gasped in surprise. "Give that back!"

It happened so fast that I was just as surprised as she was. But I didn't give it back. I tore out of the room.

"Brian!" yelled Nora.

I ran down the back stairs, out the back door, and into the yard. I wasn't sure if I really wanted to see what she was writing in that notebook or if I just wanted to make her mad—mission accomplished on that. But when she came flying out the back door, I realized I'd made a big mistake.

She was a lot faster than I'd expected. And she looked mad enough to fight.

I was trapped. The only easy escape routes were through the house or through the gate into the side yard, and Nora was between me and both of them. But there was one other option. Holding the notebook in my left hand, I ran toward the place where the fence went behind Uncle Gary's garden shed. I grabbed the top of the fence with my right hand, took two steps up the wall of the shed, and pushed off.

I fell when I landed and looked back to see Nora holding on to the top of the fence, wedging the toes of her sneakers into the chain-link diamonds.

"*You will give my notebook back,*" she snarled.

I didn't think Nora would actually go over the fence. After all, it was against the rules. But from the look on her face, she was ready to follow me to the South Pole if I could run that far.

I scrambled up what Uncle Gary called the berm and down the other side, going so fast that it was hard to stay on my feet. Nora came over the top as I crashed into the forest, her shadow stretching out toward me like a giant pointing finger.

“Give it back!” she demanded.

“No!” I said.

I felt stupid for taking the notebook, but it was too late now. Nora looked like she really wanted to clobber me. My plan was to outrun her, find my way back to the house, leave the notebook on the table, and then hide until she cooled off.

I blasted into the bushes, weaving in and out of trees and jumping over fallen trunks. Nora was right behind me. Wasn’t she getting tired? I was panting, my heart was pounding, and even worse, I had gotten a mouthful of gnats that I tried to spit out without slowing down.

Suddenly, I recognized where I was. This was where I saw the goblin-pig. I was in the middle of wondering if it could still be nearby, and whether I should be worried, when I tripped over my own feet and fell flat on my face. The green notebook slipped out of my hands. Its pages flapped like a wounded bird as it flew through the air and got caught in a tree.

Nora jogged past me but couldn’t reach it. She bent her knees and jumped—once, twice, then three times—but her fingers barely rustled the leaves of the branch she wanted.

I sat up and watched while she searched the clearing until she found a long stick. She whacked the branch with the stick, over and over, making it swing back and forth, but the notebook was stuck tight.

"Argh!" groaned Nora, swinging the stick one more time with all her might.

The notebook fell into my lap, open to a page covered in cursive. I couldn't help myself.

This is a story about a girl who traveled the world, I read. *Who knew the rules and when to break them, who met a boy who—*

That was as far as I got.

"STOP READING!" shouted Nora, yanking her notebook out of my hands.

"I'm sorry," I said. "I didn't mean to . . . well, I meant to, but . . . I didn't know it was a diary."

"It's not a diary," said Nora. "I am writing a novel. It's *fiction*. And you are not allowed to read it."

She started walking.

I got up and followed her. "A novel? That's cool."

Nora ignored me.

"What's it about? Well, actually, I guess I know what it's about. Is it going to be published someday? Because, if it is, you won't be able to keep me from reading it then. I'll just buy a copy and—"

"I wish you would just go home," said Nora over her shoulder. Her voice didn't sound mad now. It sounded small and kind of sad.

"Believe me, I would if I could," I said bitterly. "This isn't exactly my idea of a summer vacation—with school, and all your dad's rules, and you hating my guts. I miss my friends and my team and my family and my house."

She walked faster. I tried to catch up and walk next to her, but branches kept hitting me in the face. Then she stopped and I bumped into her back. She pushed me, annoyed, so I pushed her back, also annoyed. Nora turned in a slow circle, studying our surroundings.

"For the record, I don't hate you," she said.

"I guess *dislike* is a better word?"

"And I don't like school, so stop bugging me about that."

I didn't believe her, but I didn't see the point in arguing.

"Okay."

"And I need your help."

"Oh, really?" I said sarcastically. "What could you possibly need my help for?"

She folded her arms across her chest. "I don't know how to get back."

"Well, what makes you think I know where I'm going?" I asked.

"Because you came out here before, on your first day. And you found your way back."

"You've never explored the woods?"

Nora shook her head.

"Not even once? How do you look out your window at a forest every day without getting even a little bit curious?"

"It's *against the rules*, Brian," she said, sounding exasperated. "And for good reason. We're completely lost."

"No, we're not," I said. "Just follow me."

I lead the way confidently, using footprints, broken twigs, and bent grass stems to guide us. Of course, I didn't tell Nora what I was doing, because I didn't want to let her in on my secret. I wanted her to think my superior sense of direction was leading us back to the house.

But soon I wasn't so sure of myself. I lost the trail, and the next time I did find another footprint, it was going the wrong way. Did the footprint even belong to us? The shoe that made it must have been bigger than either of ours. A lot bigger.

I changed direction anyway, ignoring the silence Nora used to show doubt in my ability as a wilderness guide. Even if there were fewer signs than before, they showed that someone had passed this way not too long ago. And, even if that someone wasn't us, someone had to be going somewhere, right?

Then I lost the trail completely. I stopped. There was no point in going on without any tracks to follow. I had just come to a very serious conclusion when Nora came right out and said it.

"Well, this is just great. I'm lost . . . and you're lost, too."

CHAPTER FIVE

THE COOLEST THING EVER

We started walking again. We had no idea where we were going, but we knew no one would ever find us if we just stayed where we were. Uncle Gary was in his office, where the window looked out on the front yard. To him, it would look like we just disappeared, leaving our half-eaten lunches on the table.

"This never would have happened if you hadn't stolen my notebook," said Nora.

"Well, we wouldn't be lost if you hadn't chased me," I said.

"We're going to be so late, and my dad is going to be furious when we get back—if we ever get back," she said. "I honestly don't know what's worse: being lost or getting found."

"Maybe we'll meet the family who owns this land," I said.

Nora shuddered. "I hope not."

We were going uphill, and the trees were getting taller and farther apart. A cool breeze made the leaves rustle with a sound like rain.

"I think we should turn around," said Nora.

She was right. We were obviously going in the wrong direction. But I was curious to see what was ahead of us. As the forest changed, even the sunlight seemed different, softer and warmer somehow.

"Let's go just a little bit farther."

A few minutes later, we came to the edge of the trees and found ourselves looking into a shallow valley.

Nora gasped. "What is *that*?"

I saw the same thing she did, but I didn't know what to say.

Below us was the strangest house I'd ever seen. At first, I wasn't even sure it *was* a house. It was made completely out of wood and had a lot of the parts houses usually have, but they weren't put together the way houses usually are. Also, it was *huge*. At least six or seven stories high, although it was hard to tell exactly because the windows seemed like they were stuck on at random and you couldn't tell where any of the floors started or ended. It was really tall on one side, really short on the other, and it seemed like it went on forever in back. It also had balconies, arches, towers, turrets, and things I didn't know what to call. It looked like a castle a kindergartner might have drawn.

Heck, it looked like a castle a kindergartner might have *made.*

A real castle would have been solid as a rock, and the giant wooden house, well . . . it wasn't. It looked like it had been piled there, not built, and would fall over the next time the wind started blowing. It slumped and sagged, and some parts had obviously fallen off without being replaced. The upper floors actually seemed to be swaying in the breeze.

And then my jaw dropped and my eyes bugged out. If you were looking at me, you would have thought I was making my zombie face, but if you saw what I was looking at, your eyes would have bugged out, too. On top of the house was a big wooden boat with a rusty red smokestack and a long rudder that creaked from side to side like a giant weather vane.

It was the coolest thing I had ever seen in my entire life.

Nora was impressed, too, in her own way.

"Wow," she said. "That has to be dangerous."

She made it sound like a bad thing. "Let's get a closer look," I said.

The tall brick wall that used to protect the property was falling down, so we found a hole and climbed over a crumbled pile of bricks and rusting iron bars. We walked through a yard where the flower beds were little jungles of weeds and wild plants. I even saw vines growing in the shapes of chairs, tables, and a swing set.

When we got closer, I could hear the creaks and groans of wood rubbing against wood. The paint had all been baked away by the sun and blasted off by the wind, and the outside walls were as gray and dry as driftwood.

In front of the house, we crossed a weed-infested gravel driveway connected to a bumpy dirt road that disappeared into the woods.

A long flight of wooden stairs led up to the front door. We stopped at the first step and looked at each other.

Nora shook her head like she was snapping out of a trance. "Well, this is all very interesting, but it's definitely time to go home. I think we should try that road."

"Go home? So you can do Summer's Cool instead of having an adventure?"

"This house must belong to the people who own the woods. My dad says we're supposed to stay away from them. They'll probably have us arrested for trespassing!"

"It looks abandoned to me."

"You can't just walk in, even if it does look like a haunted house." She shuddered. "*Especially* if it looks like a haunted house."

"I'm going to ring the doorbell," I said. "If someone lives here, they can tell us how to get home. If it's abandoned, we'll take a look inside."

"You will not!" said Nora.

But she didn't turn to go. And the way she said the words, it sounded like she was curious enough to wait and watch while I did it.

I put one foot on the lowest step. It made a low creak,

like a bow drawn across two strings of a cello. Taking a deep breath, I went up the steps to a soundtrack of creaks, squeaks, and seesaw notes.

At the top, I reached for the doorbell and stopped. Where the button should have been, two twisted, wicked-looking wires stuck out, probably waiting to zap me with a thousand volts.

I decided to knock instead. Making a fist, I gave three short thumps with my knuckles, swearing when the third one gave me a splinter.

My knocking seemed to make almost no noise at all, but the door cracked open.

When I looked back at Nora, she was shaking her head.

"No!" she hissed.

"Why not?"

"I don't know! Because!"

I debated for a second—*go home or go inside?*—but only a second. *Go inside* was always going to win. I shrugged at Nora, pushed the door open wide, and stepped into the house.

"Hello?" I called. "Is anybody home?"

My voice disappeared without an echo. When my eyes got used to the dim light, I saw a room that looked like a place where they would have had sword fights in a black-and-white movie. It was almost as big as my gym at school, and everything was made of dark wood and old brass, from the grand staircase leading up to the balcony to the twenty or so doors lining the walls. There was a huge table piled with letters and packages, a tall grandfather clock, and so much stuff on the walls I could hardly believe it: stuffed animal heads, paintings of ships and people in funny clothes, giant insects in glass boxes, glittering geodes, and shelves of ancient books. Whoever lived there could have charged admission because everything looked like it belonged in a museum.

Everything, that is, except for the skateboard in the middle of the room.

There was another set of creaks and squeaks, like a violin player attacked by bats, as Nora came up the steps behind me.

"I thought you didn't want to come in," I teased her.

"I *don't*," said Nora. "I just . . . didn't want to be alone out there."

I turned and shouted into the house. "HELLO!"

"Shh!" said Nora. "Somebody might hear you!"

"That's the idea—look." I pointed at the skateboard. "Someone lives here. And they have a kid."

We both listened for a reply. But the next sound we heard came from behind us, outside the house: a revving engine. We looked out the door and saw a white van with tinted windows come out of the forest, bouncing along the bumpy road like a boat on the ocean.

"Quick!" said Nora. She pushed me inside, followed, and shut the door. Caught off balance, I fell over—and Nora, as she turned around, tripped and fell on top of me. Untangling ourselves, we scrambled to our feet and crouched behind the door.

"If they're coming home, shouldn't we wait outside?" I whispered.

"If they see us come out, they'll think we're thieves," she whispered back.

"So why did you close the door?"

"*Shh!*"

Staring at the peeling wallpaper on either side of the entrance, with the cavernous room behind us, we listened as the van came to a stop and a door slammed. A grown-up's feet thumped up the front steps.

Four loud knocks boomed on the big wooden door. Then, without warning, a rusty mail slot in the middle of the door opened and a thin white envelope came flying through.

The corner of the envelope hit me right in the eye. I yelped. Nora elbowed me in the ribs, which made me yelp again, and then clamped her hand over my mouth. This did a better job of keeping me quiet because now I couldn't breathe.

Floorboards creaked on the porch. Whoever was out there was leaning closer and listening.

"You're in there, aren't you?" said a man's voice.

Nora held her breath—and mine, too. I tried pulling her fingers off my mouth, but it was like they were glued on.

"Answer the door!" said the voice, angry now, and the door boomed again with more knocks. Then, just when I thought I was about to black out, the knocking stopped. "I'll be back," muttered the visitor. "I'll be back, and I won't be alone. You won't be able to ignore me then!"

We heard the steps creak as the visitor went back down them. The van door slammed, the engine started, and whoever it was drove away.

Nora finally let go of my face. She exhaled and I inhaled. Dusty air never tasted so sweet.

"We almost got caught, thanks to you," said Nora.

"If he had stood there any longer, you would have had to call an ambulance for me," I said. "But at least it wasn't someone who lives here. I wonder what he was so mad about."

We were sitting next to a large pile of envelopes, all of them exactly like the one that had just flown through the mail slot, all of them unopened. I guessed that they got pushed off to the side every time the door opened. Whoever lived in the house had been ignoring their mail for a long time.

I picked up the envelope that poked me. The word *URGENT* was stamped on it in red ink. It was addressed to *Homeowner, 1 Matchstick Lane*, and was from *City of Boring*. Which didn't explain anything.

We both stood up. I couldn't decide which idea was dumber: going back outside or exploring the house.

"We'll wait five minutes to make sure the van is gone," said Nora, "and then we'll go, too."

We started snooping around the big entrance hall, Nora still holding her green notebook in one hand. There was dust on everything—everything except the skateboard. But some parts of the room were dustier than others. There were footprints in the dust, and I recognized some of the paperbacks in the bookcases as ones I'd read. The house definitely wasn't abandoned.

Nora went to the far end of the room and stood in front of a fireplace that was taller than she was. Above it, out of her reach, was an old, double-barreled shotgun sitting in a giant pair of antlers, its stock and barrel all scratched and worn. I wondered if it still worked.

Then we heard new noises, this time coming from inside the house: running feet, a yell, and then banging. Something was happening upstairs.

"Let's go—*now*!" said Nora.

Going now was probably a good idea. But my feet didn't lead me to the front door. They led me to the foot of the grand staircase, where a frayed red carpet was held in place by tarnished brass rods.

The running feet thumped closer. Suddenly, a boy appeared at the top of the stairs and jumped down them a half-dozen steps at a time before skidding to a stop between me and Nora. He was a medium-sized kid with blond hair sticking out in all directions like satellite antennae. He had a grin on his face, and even though we were surprised to see *him*, he didn't look surprised to see *us*. He was holding a tennis racket.

"Hi!" he said. "I'm Cosmo van Dash. Who are you?"

"I'm Brian," I said.

"And I'm Nora," she said.

I blinked, not sure I believed my eyes: Nora had smiled. It was just a small smile, but I had never seen her do that before. It made her look weird, like she was an actress playing herself in a made-for-TV movie.

"It's great to meet you two," said Cosmo. "We don't get many kids around here."

Nora started backing up toward the door. "I'm so sorry. We were going to ring the doorbell, but there wasn't a doorbell, so we knocked, but—"

"Are you travelers?" he interrupted. "Runaways? Or are you on an adventure?"

"We're just lost," I said. "We're trying to get back to Boring."

Cosmo hardly seemed to be listening. His eyes were darting back and forth like he'd just chugged a two-liter bottle of caffeinated soda. I thought I heard a buzzing sound and wondered if it was coming from him.

"Why would you want to do that?" he asked, and then, without waiting for an answer, added, "Did you bring anything with you?"

"Anything like what?" asked Nora.

"Tennis rackets, lacrosse sticks, croquet mallets, cricket bats—anything heavier than a Wiffle bat."

"We didn't bring anything," I said. "But like I said, we really weren't expecting to be here."

Croquet mallets? Cricket bats? What was he talking about?

I heard an angry, buzzing sound behind me, like a flying weed whacker.

"Duck!" said Cosmo.

"What?" I said.

"DUCK!" yelled Cosmo, holding his tennis racket in two hands and putting it on his shoulder like a baseball player getting ready to swing.

Nora screamed. I ducked. And Cosmo swung the tennis racket.

CHAPTER SIX

WASPS!

There was a *WHOOF!* and then a *WHAP!* and then the buzzing sound fizzled away up the stairs like a remote-control plane with a short circuit.

I turned to look but was too late. Nora had turned as white as a piece of notebook paper.

"What the heck was that?"

"A wasp," said Cosmo. "We're infested. They're upstairs—well, most of them. Part of the problem is that I don't know where all of them are."

Nora headed for the door, and I started to follow her. Going outside when the wasps were inside seemed like a great idea. But Cosmo stayed put.

"Where are you going?" he asked.

"Away from the wasps, obviously," said Nora.

"Where are *you* going?" I asked Cosmo.

He put one foot on the stairs. "I have to catch them. But you guys can help . . . if you want."

Nora shook her head violently, and his face fell.

"I'm coming," I heard myself say.

"Brian!" said Nora. "It's too dangerous, and we're already ridiculously late for school. We need to go back *right now*."

At that point, I would have rather been stung by a giant wasp than sit down for Summer's Cool. Besides, Cosmo seemed so nice, and it sounded like he really wanted our help.

"Suit yourself," I told her, climbing the stairs.

Nora looked at us and then at the front door. She was afraid of the wasps, obviously, but I knew she was also afraid to go back through the forest alone. And, from the way she had smiled at Cosmo—actually *smiled*—I had a feeling she thought he was . . . cute. *Disgusting.*

By the time we reached the second floor, Nora must have made up her mind, because she was following us.

"Are you sure we shouldn't call an exterminator instead?" she asked.

"North American exterminators don't have any experience with South American wasps," Cosmo explained.

Realizing that I was still holding the recently delivered letter, I slipped it into my pocket. I'd put it back on the pile as soon as I had a chance. I didn't want Cosmo to think I had stolen his family's mail.

Cosmo moved so fast we had to run to keep up. From the balcony overlooking the entrance, we went into a narrow hallway where the walls were lined with old books. As we ran, the floor sloped upward and the ceiling sloped downward until it was only a few inches above Nora, the tallest of the three of us.

"You see, they're not just any old wasps. They're giant wasps—" began Cosmo.

"*Giant* wasps?" interrupted Nora.

"—from the Amazon—"

"How did they get here?" I asked.

"My father brought them," said Cosmo, hopping down into a little room crowded with big, comfy-looking armchairs.

"Your *father*?" we both asked simultaneously, trying to imagine why anyone's dad would bring home wasps from a business trip.

"Yes. Dashiell van Dash." He waited a few seconds, like he expected us to recognize the name. "You know, *the* Dashiell van Dash."

Nora and I looked at each other.

"The famous explorer?" Cosmo went on. "The man who discovered the underground pyramids of Madagascar? The first man to navigate from pole to pole in a bicycle-powered hot air balloon? The only person to ever survive a fistfight with the abominable snowman? You've never *heard* of him?"

"No, I haven't," said Nora.

"Me neither," I admitted.

"People don't read as much as they should," muttered

Cosmo before taking a deep breath and stepping into another hallway. "Anyway, he brought these back from the Amazon, but it was completely by accident. My father would never relocate a species from its native habitat on purpose. Apparently, a wasp queen laid some eggs in one of his packing crates. By the time the crates were delivered, the larvae were hatching. There really are a lot of them, and we have to find them all because they're wood burrowers."

Nora looked around nervously while we walked, like she expected the giant wasps to attack us at any moment. "But why doesn't your dad take care of this? Where is he?"

"He went away again without unpacking, and the wasps just started chewing their way out of the crates. I'm not actually sure where he is now. Adventuring isn't like working in an office, where you know what's going to happen every day."

As we made two left turns and then climbed a flight of stairs, I thought about my dad in Antarctica. The difference between me and Cosmo, though, was that he hadn't been kicked out of *his* home while his dad was on an adventure.

"So he left you here alone?" I asked.

"Of course not," said Cosmo. "I'm only eleven. My uncles live here, too."

"So where are they?" asked Nora.

"They're around somewhere. They have more important things to do than follow me around all day."

"Where do you go to school?"

Cosmo paused at the top of the stairs and looked back.

"Oh, I don't go to school. My father says I'm enrolled in the school of life."

"That's not *fair*," I said. Cosmo would never have to waste his time with educational software.

"My father says life isn't fair," agreed Cosmo.

He led us around a corner into a hallway where the walls weren't parallel, the floor slanted to one side, and the ceiling sagged like an elephant had been doing tricks upstairs. There were doors on one side and windows on the other. Through the windows, I could see treetops and a wide, curving river.

Curious about what was behind the nearest door, I turned the handle.

"DON'T OPEN THAT!" Cosmo pushed it closed and shoved me out of the way. "There's a fifty-foot drop behind it and you could be killed."

"Why would a house have a fifty-foot drop behind an ordinary-looking door?" demanded Nora.

"Castle, not house," Cosmo corrected her. "We call it the Matchstick Castle. Because, well—"

"Because it looks like a castle made out of wood and the address is on Matchstick Lane," I interrupted. "That's perfect!"

Cosmo smiled.

"Well, why does your *castle* have a fifty-foot drop behind an ordinary-looking door?" repeated Nora.

Cosmo folded his arms and sighed. "I'll answer all your

questions later. I promise. Now, how do you think we should catch the wasps?"

Nora looked shocked. "But . . . don't you *know*?"

"Why would I know how to catch giant Amazonian wasps?"

"Well, wasps love picnics," I said, thinking out loud. "Especially at the end of summer. When we have a picnic on Labor Day weekend, the wasps always ruin it."

"That's good!" said Cosmo.

"They also like soda," I added. "One time, my friend Wilhelmina got stung on the tongue because she took a drink of soda and a wasp had crawled into the can."

"You see," said Cosmo, "that's the kind of thinking we need."

I smiled at Nora, but she just stared at me with cold reptilian eyes. She wasn't used to getting outthought, especially by me.

"But how does Brian's friend getting stung on the tongue by an ordinary American wasp help us catch giant Amazonian wasps?" asked Nora.

"It doesn't," said Cosmo. "At least, I don't think so. But the only way to solve a problem is to start brainstorming."

Suddenly, I heard something that sounded like a bad marching band playing a one-note song on beat-up kazoos.

"Do you hear that?"

Everyone listened.

The kazoos were getting louder fast, as if the band had started running.

"They're coming!" Cosmo had barely said the words when a huge wasp—its yellow-and-black body as big as Wilhelmina's soda can—flew down the hallway as fast as a bullet.

Nora screamed.

But Cosmo jumped in front of her, raised his tennis racket over his head like a professional player serving a ball, and smashed the wasp back the way it came. Down the hall, the kazoo sound got wobbly, like the marching band was stumbling over speed bumps.

"Quick!" yelled Cosmo. "Behind that door!"

"I thought you said there's a fifty-foot drop behind it," I said.

"Not that one—the one next to it!"

I opened the door Cosmo pointed at and stared into darkness. For all I knew, this one had a hundred-foot drop. But falling down a hole still sounded better than getting stung to death by giant wasps. Taking a deep breath, I stepped inside.

"GRAB THE POLE!" shouted Cosmo.

I was already falling forward when I saw a fireman's pole in front of me. I wrapped my arms around it and held tight, my momentum spinning me around the pole as I slid down.

Looking up, I saw Nora reach out and hug the pole. Then Cosmo followed, pulling the door shut behind him.

I whizzed past a closed door, a crawl space filled with spiderwebs, another door—I think—and then my feet hit the ground so hard my knees buckled. Before I could get out of the way, Nora landed on top of me and Cosmo landed on top of her.

Above us, the angry buzzing of the wasps sounded like a vibrating cell phone. It was so dark, all I could see was dimly colored spots.

"Whew!" said Cosmo.

"How do we get out of here?" asked Nora.

I would have said something, too, if they weren't both squishing the air out of my lungs.

Cosmo and Nora were trying to stand up, but it wasn't easy. The walls were so close that it was like we were wedged into a chimney. They couldn't move without stepping on me—but at least Cosmo apologized.

I might have accidentally elbowed Nora while I fought my way to my feet.

"Please tell me we don't have to climb back up the pole," I begged Cosmo.

"No, there's a door. A hidden one, so I have to find it first."

Cosmo wriggled around, first high, then low, then reached between me and Nora.

Nora giggled.

"What's so funny?" I asked.

"Nothing." She giggled again. "That tickles!"

Smiling, giggling—what was next? Maybe she'd start singing and dancing.

"Sorry," said Cosmo. "I'm looking for . . . There it is!"

I felt Cosmo's arm go down, then up. I heard a click, and then the wall behind me slid open, and we tumbled into a well-lit room and landed on a deep, dusty carpet. Naturally, I was on the bottom again.

"The library," said Cosmo, coughing. "If we can't find an answer here, then we're really in trouble."

CHAPTER SEVEN

PRIMARY SOURCES

Nora and Cosmo sat on a couch with a thick encyclopedia between them. Cosmo was studying the articles carefully, but Nora barely even looked at them. She was studying Cosmo like he was the first boy she'd ever seen in her life. She was fascinated and I was nauseated.

Trying to ignore them, I searched the shelves for books on insects and extermination. We had been working for an hour and still hadn't found anything. At any moment, I expected to hear the angry-kazoo sound of the wasps again.

If I wasn't so nervous about the inch-long stingers of giant Amazonian wasps, I might have been enjoying myself. I'd rather play soccer than read any day, but the van Dash family library wasn't like any library I'd seen before. It filled room after room, and every wall of every room was covered from top to bottom with books, some of them hundreds of years old. There were comfortable couches, chairs, and footstools everywhere and lots of different lamps and tables. There were stacks of books all over the floor, too, like the Matchstick Castle's librarian had run out of space on the shelves. Some of the stacks were almost as tall as I was.

There was an old-fashioned card catalog, but it wasn't very helpful. Under the subject heading *Wasps*, for example, there was this title: *Wasps: Symbolic Importance of Aculeata in the Aboriginal Arts of South America.*

Then, instead of a call number, the book's location was written in pencil: *On the third or fourth shelf above the spot where Roald spilled the bowl of Artillery punch at Christmas.*

Cosmo said the punch must have been spilled before he was born and he had no idea where it happened.

"My uncle Kingsley keeps the card catalog in order, but unfortunately, he went missing about a year ago. You've heard of him, of course—Kingsley van Dash, the famous author?"

I shook my head. Of course I hadn't, just like I hadn't heard of Dashiell van Dash, the famous explorer.

"Actually, that rings a bell," Nora said.

"Maybe you've read his book," said Cosmo hopefully.

"No," she said. "But I think I've seen it somewhere before."

"It's no use!" Cosmo slammed the encyclopedia shut. "The Latin classification, biomes, and reproductive habits of wasps don't tell us anything about how to catch them. Encyclopedias just aren't practical."

I kept looking at the shelves, hoping to find something that could save us. Then I spotted a beat-up old book called *Gadding about in Darkest Amazonia* by someone named Percival "Harry" Pratchett, C.B.E.

Cosmo's wasps were from the Amazon. Maybe Pratchett had run into them, too. Pulling the book off the shelf, I turned to the index. I found headings for *Ants, antagonizing*; *Bugs, bothersome*; *Insects, irritating*; and *Wasps, woefully large*.

When I found the right page, I started reading out loud: "'After making camp late one afternoon, with victuals and cordials having been eagerly consumed, we were troubled by the sound of what appeared to be poorly played reed instruments. The noise, we soon discovered, was made by wasps of a size heretofore unrecorded by previous explorers. Several of our company fell prey to fatal stings before it was noticed that the wasps feared to enter the ambit of the campfire. The smoke! I deduced doggedly. We fashioned crude incendiaries with green bush-wood and were able to hold the insects at bay until they retreated at nightfall. We broke camp before dawn and left the area posthaste.'

"What's an incendiary?" I asked.

"He means a torch," said Nora.

"That's it!" shouted Cosmo.

"What's it?" I asked.

"The wasps hate smoke, so we'll smoke them out," said Cosmo. "Well done, Brian! We're going to make a good team."

I closed the book, feeling pretty good about myself. But I still wasn't sure we'd solved the problem.

"And how will we make the smoke?" Nora asked skeptically.

"Making smoke is no problem at all," answered Cosmo. "Follow me!"

Cosmo took off at top speed, and we had to run to keep up again. Leaving the library, we raced down a hall, around a corner, up a small hill, and stopped in a dining room where the table was set for a fancy dinner—under a thick layer of dust.

The table was so long it could have been used as a bowling lane. And there must have been two dozen pieces of everything, from plates and bowls to three different kinds of forks. I didn't know what half of the utensils were for.

"This silver needs a good polish," said Nora. She picked up a big wine goblet and looked inside. Then she shrieked and threw it halfway across the room.

Cosmo raised his eyebrows, but he didn't seem mad.

"Sorry," she muttered. "Spider."

"We usually eat in the kitchen," Cosmo explained.

Then, while Nora fetched the goblet and I counted the salt and pepper shakers—there were twenty-four of each—he walked to the far end of the room.

When we looked up, he was gone.

I scanned the room: ugly wallpaper, old pictures of funny-looking people, and no Cosmo.

"Where are you?" I called.

"Follow my voice!" called Cosmo. "It's an optical illusion."

When we got closer, we could see a small partition sticking out, its wallpaper perfectly matched to the rest of the room. Behind the partition was an opening in the wall about three feet by three feet. And, curled up in the opening, was Cosmo.

"It's a dumbwaiter," he explained. "Back when there were fancy dinners here, they could make the food appear as if by magic."

"How long ago was that?" I asked.

"No idea," he said. "Lower me down and then you two come after me."

The dumbwaiter was basically a large box, open on the side facing the room, that could be raised and lowered with ropes and pulleys. Everything was so perfectly balanced that I could lower Cosmo down using only one hand.

When I felt the rope jiggle and heard Cosmo call, I raised the dumbwaiter again. This time, I climbed in while Nora held the rope. The old wooden box was worn smooth and stained where food had spilled. Like most of the house, it smelled dry and dusty.

I plunged into darkness, landing with a thump that rattled my teeth like dice in a cup. Groaning, I crawled out into a big kitchen.

"You let go of the rope!" I yelled up at Nora.

"Sorry!" she yelled back, not sounding sorry at all.

Cosmo raised the box back up to Nora and held the rope while she got in.

"I can do it," I told him.

Cosmo stepped aside and I took the rope. I felt it go taut from Nora's weight. Then, when she called, "Lower me down!" I let go. The pulleys rattled, the box fell, and Nora landed with a bang and a scream. She climbed out slowly, moving like she was ninety years old and everything hurt.

"Isn't there an easier way downstairs?" demanded Nora, glaring at me.

"Yes, but stairs aren't nearly as fun as a dumbwaiter," Cosmo answered.

"I guess that depends on who's holding the rope," she said.

With cracked white tile and old-fashioned cabinets, the kitchen reminded me of a mad scientist's laboratory, and the big table in the middle of the room was definitely long enough for Frankenstein's monster. There wasn't a refrigerator, but there was a big wooden door, held shut by a rusty metal latch, labeled ICE. And I guessed they cooked their meals on the giant, old-fashioned stove in the corner.

Cosmo lifted an iron cooking plate on the stove top and shook his head. Then he opened a low door in its side, looked in, and nodded.

"Wait here," he said. He left the room and came back a few minutes later carrying a metal pan with a hinged lid and a long wooden handle, an old-fashioned fan with a flimsy cage, a thick coil of yellow extension cord, and, of course, his tennis racket.

"Let me guess—we're having a yard sale," I said.

Cosmo looked at me like he didn't know what a yard sale was. His family had probably never had one.

"Please ignore my cousin," said Nora. "What's the plan?"

"It's really quite simple," he explained, putting everything on the big table. "I'll use this old bed warmer to make smoke. We can use the smoke to make the wasps go where we want them by directing it with the fan. If there isn't an outlet nearby, then we'll use the extension cord. And we still have the tennis racket in case any wasps get past the smoke. But I'm going to need your help."

I stared at him, trying to picture exactly how it was going to work.

"Where are we chasing the wasps *to*?" asked Nora.

"I want to put them back in the packing crate they came out of."

"I thought they ate the crate," I said.

"Just made some holes. We can put the crate in a metal chest."

I picked up the tennis racket. It *did* look kind of like a giant flyswatter. "And then we'll kill them?"

Cosmo shook his head. "It's not these wasps' fault they accidentally ended up in the wrong hemisphere. We'll just pack them up and ship them back to Brazil."

"Wait a minute," said Nora, drumming her fingers on the table. "The wasps are a danger because they might eat the house, which is made of wood. But aren't you creating an even greater danger to the house?"

Cosmo looked at her, not understanding.

"If you're making smoke, you're making fire, too, or at least something very, very hot. We need a fire extinguisher."

With a huge sigh, Cosmo dropped the supplies on the floor and took off again. He was gone longer this time, but when he came back, he was dragging a tall, copper-covered fire extinguisher that had turned sea green with age.

"Brian, can you can carry this and the tennis racket?" he asked, panting.

"I think so," I told him.

Without waiting for Nora to come up with any more objections, Cosmo used a ladle to scoop coals from the stove into the pan of the bed warmer. The coals glowed red-hot but hardly smoked at all. Then he opened a large can labeled LAPSANG SOUCHONG, shook some tea leaves out into a bowl, and splashed them with hot water from the faucet.

"I think we're ready," he said. "Nora, can you handle the fan?"

Nora had been carrying her notebook all this time. Setting it down on a counter, she picked up the fan and stared at it. The spaces in the cage around its blades were big enough to put her hand through. She shook her head in a kind of diagonal nod that could have meant anything. I guess Cosmo thought it meant yes.

I nodded straight up and down. I didn't want it to look like Nora was braver than me.

"Good," said Cosmo. "And now, my friends, let's go get those wasps!"

He dumped fistfuls of wet tea leaves on the hot coals. There was an angry hiss and then smoke started pouring out of the pan.

"Follow me!" shouted Cosmo, and he rushed out of the room.

CHAPTER EIGHT

BATTLING THE WASPS

Hanging the loops of the extension cord over one shoulder, Nora ran after Cosmo with the fan. I could hardly lift the fire extinguisher, never mind run with it. Cradling it in my arms like a big metal baby and holding the tennis racket under my chin, I clomped after them with the water sloshing back and forth inside the metal canister.

Smoke filled the hallway, making it almost impossible to see Cosmo and Nora ahead of me. But as long as I followed the smoke, I figured I couldn't get lost. After all, Cosmo knew where he was going.

"Won't this set off the smoke detector?" coughed Nora.

"Smoke . . . detector?" repeated Cosmo. From the way he said the words, it was clear he'd never heard them used together.

It didn't take long to find the wasps. Their angry buzzing grew louder as we got closer.

"I think they're swarming!" he shouted. "That's good!"

I didn't think swarms of regular-sized wasps were good, and swarms of giant Amazonian wasps were especially not good. On the other hand, I was last in line, and it made me feel better knowing the wasps would probably sting Nora first.

The buzzing got louder, like they were warning each other that we were coming. Did wasps have noses? Could they smell the smoke?

"Quick!" shouted Cosmo. "Plug in the fan, Nora!"

Nora looked around frantically. "I can't find an outlet. It's too smoky."

The smoke was drifting back toward us, making it hard to see. My burning eyes and clogged lungs made me feel like I was standing on the wrong side of a campfire.

"They're trying to escape!" he said.

There was an angry buzz as a dark shape emerged from the smoke. Without thinking, I dropped the fire extinguisher and swung the tennis racket. Direct hit! The wasp bounced off the wall and pinballed back up the hall.

"Good shot," said Cosmo. "But try not to hit too hard. We don't want to hurt them."

Have you ever tried hitting a giant wasp delicately with a tennis racket?

Three more approached. I caught the first one with a forehand, the second one with a backhand, and the third one with a volley that was barely strong enough to send it the other way.

"What happens if we get stung?" I panted.

"The sting is usually fatal in adolescents," said Cosmo cheerfully, "so be careful."

The smoke was so thick that soon I wasn't going to be able to tell if I was hitting wasps or Cosmo's and Nora's heads—I didn't know how Cosmo's plan could possibly work.

Then a cool breeze tickled the back of my neck as a draft of air wafted up the hallway and parted the smoke. It must have come from deep in the house, because there were no windows in sight.

There was a shout from Nora. "I see an outlet!"

The fan rattled to life, its blades spinning slowly at first, then faster and faster as she adjusted the speed. She stood behind Cosmo, and the smoke began to drift forward. As the hallway cleared, I could see for the first time how many wasps there were. A few were flying in circles, but most of them were clustered along one wall, their writhing bodies packed so tightly it was hard to tell them apart. They seemed to be working on something.

I could hear them chewing.

"They're collecting wood pulp for a nest," Cosmo told us. "If we can't get rid of them, they'll destroy the house."

But the smoke was already beginning to bug the wasps.

Now that I wasn't swatting them, I was able to get a good look at their huge alien eyes; hunchbacked, honey-colored thoraxes; and swollen, all-black abdomens. Their stingers were the size of toothpicks, and I could see glistening drops of venom at the points.

Remembering how Wilhelmina got stung, I realized that these freaky flying insects would never in a million years fit inside a soda can—and they probably didn't drink soda, anyway. They probably ate the cans.

Some of them started swirling angrily around the hall in twos and threes, buzzing closer and closer and making Nora and me shrink back.

The smoke made them mad, but they didn't want to fly into it. When Cosmo took a step toward them, the wasps moved back just a little bit. And when he took another step, they moved back a little more. We moved slowly down the hall, herding them ahead of us. By now I was dragging the fire extinguisher with my left hand so I could hold the tennis racket with my right.

"How far do we have to go?" asked Nora, letting out more of the extension cord.

"Just a couple hundred feet," said Cosmo. "We're very close to the room with the crate."

"How long is the extension cord?"

"Fifty yards, I think."

I tried to do the math in my head. One yard was equal to thirty-six inches, which was three feet. We had three times fifty feet of cord to cover two hundred feet, which meant . . . under the circumstances, it was very hard to think. I imagined Darren and Dara waving their arms at me: *We're waiting!*

But Nora could probably do math while walking across hot coals. "We're going to run out of extension cord," she announced. "We'll be fifty feet short, if Cosmo's estimate is correct."

"Too late to stop now," he said.

As we advanced down the hallway, I kept looking for another outlet. No luck. The house was so old that I was amazed there were any outlets at all. The coils of yellow cord were slipping off Nora's shoulder quickly—there were only a half dozen left. Soon we wouldn't be able to go any farther.

Even worse, the smoke, which at first billowed out of the bed warmer like it would never stop, was now getting thin and wispy. And with less smoke, the wasps were less afraid of us. They weren't moving down the hallway as fast as before and had started circling closer and closer to Cosmo.

I gripped the tennis racket tighter. In a moment, I would have to swat the wasps like I was trying to win at Wimbledon. Meanwhile, my left arm was ready to fall off from lugging the fire extinguisher.

"Almost out of extension cord," warned Nora.

"Almost out of smoke," confirmed Cosmo.

The wasps swirled with even more energy, as though they knew they were about to have the advantage. The noise got louder. All those wings started beating the smoke back toward Cosmo, who coughed, lost his grip on the handle of the bed warmer, and spilled gray coals onto the wooden floor.

The wasps flew toward us.

And then it hit me—not a wasp, but an idea. Dropping the tennis racket, I pulled the fire extinguisher upright. I grabbed the rubber hose with one hand and the wheel on top with the other. But when I tried to turn the wheel, it didn't move.

A couple of wasps zoomed past my head and down the hall.

There were raised letters on the side of canister: FOR FIRE, TURN BOTTOM UP. Guessing that didn't mean *my* bottom, I turned the fire extinguisher upside down. I heard a *THUNK* and a furious fizzing inside as water started streaming out of the hose.

"Duck!" I yelled.

Cosmo and Nora ducked.

The water came out in a fine spray, the kind old men used to water their little lawns back home in Boston. I waved the hose back and forth.

The wasps didn't like the water at all. They retreated, and I advanced past Nora and Cosmo.

"Which door?" I shouted.

"Last one on the left!" Cosmo yelled back.

I marched ahead, forcing the angry wasps down the hall-way and into the open door. I was tempted to just slam the door but remembered what Cosmo had said about the crate. I followed the wasps into the room, soaking everything inside of it—books, papers, and paintings—and forced the wet, unhappy insects toward a large wooden packing crate. It wasn't easy. Even though the wasps hated the water, they were confused and disoriented and I had to circle the room three times before they had all piled on top of each other in the box, burrowing toward the center of the pile and trying to escape the downpour.

A few wasps, too waterlogged to fly, twitched in puddles on the floor. Carefully grabbing them by their middles to avoid their stingers and jaws, Cosmo tossed them inside the box and then slammed the wooden lid shut.

Panting and feeling a little shaky, I closed the valve on the fire extinguisher just as the last of the water dribbled out.

"Well, that was close," said Cosmo. "Good thinking, Brian!"

"That crate has more holes than Swiss cheese," declared Nora.

Cosmo thumped his hand on an old metal sea chest lying against one wall. "And that's why we'll put it inside this. Lend me a hand, will you?"

We helped him take everything out of the chest—boxes filled with microscope slides and specimen jars, an animal skull wrapped in cheesecloth, and weird bundles covered with leaves. Then, straining, all three of us lowered the box of wasps into the chest before closing the lid and snapping the latches. Cosmo used a hammer and nail to make air holes so the wasps wouldn't suffocate.

"What will they eat?" I asked.

"Well, the crate, but that's mostly fiber and they'll need protein, too. I'll throw in some steaks. But we'd better send it by air freight to make sure they're healthy when they arrive."

I looked around the room. It was soaked. The hallway outside was soaked, too, and the house reeked of smoke. It was an epic, disastrous, once-in-a-lifetime mess.

"Boy, are we going to be in trouble," said Nora gloomily.

"Why?" asked Cosmo.

Nora waved her arms at the wreckage around us. "Because . . . because . . . well, *everything*."

"But we saved the Matchstick Castle," Cosmo pointed out. Then he sniffed. "Though it is sort of smoky and damp in here. We'd better air it out."

He pulled back heavy curtains from a cracked and dirty window. After banging its frame so hard I was sure he would break the glass, he was finally able to force it open. Smoke drifted out, and we heard a questioning shout from below. Cosmo laughed as he waved to someone outside.

"No!" he replied. "It's not on fire!"

Turning to us, he pointed out the window. "That's my uncle Montague."

I looked out the window and saw a man making his way toward the house.

"And who might you be?" he called out in a friendly voice.

"Brian!" I shouted.

"And Nora!" shouted Nora over my shoulder.

"Very nice to meet you both!"

He was having a hard time walking, which might have been because he was carrying a big, dead, furry animal across his shoulders.

We followed Cosmo to the kitchen, arriving just in time to see Montague come through the back door and drop the animal on the wooden table with a thud. I recognized it as the thing that had nearly run me over in the forest on my first day in Boring. Its fur was stiff, and it had a whiskery snout and razor-sharp tusks.

"So we are not to worry about the smoke that was pouring out the windows of our ancestral family home?" Montague asked Cosmo. "Where there was smoke, there was not—at least in this instance—fire?"

"No," Cosmo told him. "Wasps."

"Ah," said Montague, like that was all he needed to know. "And you have new friends, I see. I'm very pleased to meet you both. Montague van Dash, Cosmo's uncle. I tend the garden, butcher the meat, and am also the chief cook and bottle washer."

He was tall and tubby, with red cheeks and a bald head. His clothes—a tweed jacket, tie, and tall rubber boots—made him look like a professor who'd accidentally gone hunting.

But Nora couldn't take her eyes off the animal on the table. "There was a wild boar in this forest?" she asked.

"There are four. Or, rather, there are now three. Some foolish person once tried to raise them as domestic livestock, and they escaped. I've been after them ever since."

"Who tried to raise them as domestic livestock?" I asked.

"I did," he said. "It was devilish hard, too."

It was impossible not to like him. He looked completely ridiculous but was so cheerful that I had the feeling he could make himself laugh just by thinking about himself. When he smiled, his eyes practically disappeared in his chubby face.

"Given that he has been living quite comfortably off the carrots, potatoes, and mushrooms in my garden, I believe this boar will taste delightful," said Montague. "Will you, Brian and Nora, do us the great honor of staying for dinner?"

"Definitely," I said.

But Nora suddenly turned pale. "What time is it?"

Cosmo looked at a cuckoo clock on the wall, but it wasn't ticking and the hands were stuck at twelve.

Montague squinted at the fading light in the window. "Early evening, I believe. Cocktail hour for some. I'd better get cooking if we're to eat before bedtime."

Nora grabbed her green notebook off the counter and turned to me. "We have to go home *right now.* We missed the whole afternoon of school and nobody knows where we are. My parents are going to be freaking out. And my dad is going to have us make up the work we missed—probably on Saturday."

I felt like she'd sprayed me with the fire extinguisher.

For the last few hours, I'd managed to completely forget about Uncle Gary and Summer's Cool.

"Could you tell us how to get back to Sixteen Sunnybright Circle?" asked Nora.

Montague made a face and shuddered like he'd just swallowed vinegar. "I'm sorry. I'm sure it's very nice, but I just don't think I'd be able to live in one of those little cookie boxes. You couldn't possibly get lost in them! But you'll find your way back quite easily if you follow the dirt road until you see a gate on the right. Pass through and follow the path beyond, which will bring you out at the end of your street."

They walked us to the front door, which took a while.

"I must insist you take a rain check," said Montague. "Come for dinner, say, next Thursday. And don't worry about the hour—we eat quite late."

"You will come back, won't you?" asked Cosmo hopefully, jumping up and balancing on the porch railing.

"Thank you for the invitation," said Nora. "And of course we'd love to come, Cosmo, but I don't know if we can. It depends on—"

"We will!" I interrupted.

Nora dragged me out the door and down the steps, and we started running up the road toward the trees. Looking over my shoulder, I could see Cosmo and Montague standing at the top of the steps, waving good-bye.

CHAPTER NINE

GROUNDED

It's bad enough that you skipped a whole afternoon of Summer's Cool. But it's *completely* unacceptable that you disappeared without telling me where you were going."

Uncle Gary may have been talking to both of us, but he was saving most of his glares for me. Aunt Jenny looked more disappointed than mad, but she obviously wasn't happy, either.

When we had come out of the woods at the newest part of Sunnybright Circle where there were half-built houses with plastic tarps flapping in the wind, we knew right away we were in deep trouble. The sun had set, the stars were coming out, and I could see flashlights bobbing up and down the sidewalks—the whole neighborhood seemed to be out looking for us.

But the thing that made me realize we were really in for

it was the police car parked in front of number sixteen. Its red and blue flashers lit up the house, and I could hear its radio crackling from all the way down the block.

Nora broke into a run. "Here we are! We're safe! Sorry!"

Everyone was happy to see us—at first. The neighbors hugged us and escorted us to Nora's house, where Uncle Gary was talking to a police officer. Aunt Jenny smothered us with more hugs, telling us how worried she'd been and in the same breath insisting that we must be starving. The police officer flashed us a reassuring smile and shook Uncle Gary's hand before heading back out to his car.

As soon as we were inside with the door closed, though, Uncle Gary's smile disappeared. He was so mad he was practically shaking. We all went into the kitchen, and while Aunt Jenny started pulling leftovers out of the fridge and putting food on plates, Nora apologized for disappearing and then I told them what had happened. I didn't expect them to believe me, but they did.

And then I wished they didn't.

"What did I say to you on Monday?" demanded Uncle Gary, glaring at me.

I glared back and didn't say anything, but Nora answered for me.

"You said we weren't supposed to go into the forest."

"That's right," said Uncle Gary. "And what else did I say?"

"Keep away from the family who owns the woods," mumbled Nora.

"And, if those two instructions were clear, what would make you think that you'd have permission to go *into their house*?"

I hate it when parents act like they're lawyers. We all knew that Nora and I were in trouble, but instead of just handing out the punishment, he had to walk us through each step like he was convincing the jury we were guilty.

"But they're so nice!" said Nora, before Uncle Gary could start his closing argument. "We only knocked on the door because we were lost and wanted to ask for directions. And then the door opened and we met their son, Cosmo."

"And he needed help, so what were we supposed to do—say no?" I added, glad that she left out the part about the white van and the letter.

"And where were Cosmo's parents?" demanded Uncle Gary.

"His dad was at work," I said, which was technically true. "I'm not sure where his mom was."

"Who leaves their kid home alone in a house full of giant wasps?"

"They didn't know about the giant wasps, actually."

"Well, what kind of person accidentally brings a box of giant wasps home with them?"

"Cosmo's uncle was in the backyard," added Nora, leaving out the fact that he had been busy shooting a wild animal. "He was so polite, and he even invited us to come back for dinner."

"I don't care if they are the nicest people in the state of Illinois," said Uncle Gary, his voice getting louder and louder until he was practically shouting. "That doesn't do me a bit of good if you both wind up in the hospital. If these wasps were even half the size you say they are, you entered a life-threatening situation the moment you went through their door. And you're lucky you weren't crushed by a falling boat on your way out!"

"Well, the important thing is that they're safe now," said Aunt Jenny, trying to calm him down.

But Uncle Gary wouldn't stop until he'd passed sentence. "You're grounded, both of you. You will stay in either the house or the yard for one week. And I expect an apology for your behavior today."

"I'm sorry, Dad," said Nora, staring at her shoes.

"I'm not," I muttered.

Uncle Gary gave me a stare cold enough to make ice cubes. "You certainly will be. This household was running smoothly until you showed up and started encouraging Nora to break the rules. You two can go to your rooms."

"What about their dinners?" asked Aunt Jenny, ready to put a plate of meatloaf and mashed potatoes in the microwave.

I didn't like meatloaf—I had never even had it before coming to Boring—but I was so hungry that even a gray slice of pressed meat looked edible.

"They can eat in their rooms while they think about what they've done," said Uncle Gary. "And no ice cream. Brian, I hope you'll feel more sorry by morning."

I *was* sorry. Sorry my dad's dream was coming true, sorry I'd been born into a family with an uncle Gary in it, sorry Illinois even existed so there could be a place like Boring. On Saturday, we were forced to make up all the school we missed on Friday, plus extra, and on Sunday I spent the day in my joke of a room, thinking of all the unpleasant things I'd like to do to Uncle Gary. If I knew how, I would have written a virus that made Darren and Dara fight to the death.

By bedtime, I'd read every comic book I brought with me and had no idea what I would do for the rest of the time I was grounded. Something interesting had finally happened, and the grown-ups were mad because we weren't inside on our computers.

Monday was the Fourth of July—not that it mattered. We didn't get to shoot off a single firework all weekend, and we certainly didn't get to go to the Boring fireworks display, even though I could hear the occasional *boom* and *crackle* in the distance. I could tell it was lame compared to the epic fireworks display over the Charles River in Boston, but still, the sounds of Independence Day only reminded me of how much freedom I'd lost.

That morning, though—a week after I arrived—I finally

got an e-mail from my dad. I had just booted up my laptop. I had a few minutes before Uncle Gary would make me log in to Summer's Cool, so I decided to check for messages.

Brian,

I feel terrible that it has taken me so long to get in touch. Please accept my apologies. I hope you weren't worried about me. Everything is fine: I am at the South Pole, hard at work. There were a few hiccups along the way, however. We were delayed in leaving Christchurch, New Zealand, due to a terrible storm. Then, finally, two whole days late, we took off. As we entered Antarctic airspace, our plane developed engine trouble and the pilot had to set us down on the ice—a crash landing! Fortunately, everybody was fine except for a few bumps and bruises. It was quite cold outside, but we had plenty of supplies in the plane, so we kept warm and waited for rescue. (Funny, really, given that we were the rescue plane!) The weather got worse and worse, but eventually we were met by some Russian researchers driving a snowcat, a funny-looking jeep with four sets of caterpillar treads instead of wheels. They took us to McMurdo Station, where we were supposed to land in the first place. After a few more days of waiting, the storm lifted and our supplies (including me) were finally delivered to the Amundsen-Scott South Pole Station on another plane that came from New Zealand. They were able to take the injured astronomer back on the return flight, so now she is in good hands and I am hard at work.

The telescope is simply amazing. The skies are so dark here I feel as though I can see forever. Because it's night all the time, I feel as though I could work all the time, too—I have to remind myself to go to bed. But I do want to make the most of this opportunity. Who knows if it will ever come again?

I was sorry to get your e-mail and to hear that you are so unhappy. I wish my long-term goal didn't have to come at the expense of your short-term happiness. If there was something I could do for you right now, I would. All I can say is try to make the best of it and remember that Uncle Gary and Aunt Jenny do love you, even if they don't show it in a way you are used to.

And I love you, too.

Dad

Reading about the plane crash, my stomach felt cold and hollow. It was a lot to think about—finding out he was okay at the same time as finding out he maybe could have died. I missed him so much. I'd have given anything to have had one of those annoying sneak-attack hugs he always gave me at breakfast.

Suddenly, it didn't seem like a good time to complain

about Uncle Gary. And at least something interesting had happened to me, too. I wrote back right away:

Dear Dad,

I'm so glad you're safe. That's crazy about the plane crash! The kids at school will never believe it. Please don't worry about me. I'm fine. I still hate it here, but at least something interesting has happened. You'll be "buzzing" when I tell you. Won't write more now because the story isn't over . . . I hope.

Love, Brian

PS Oh yeah, I'm grounded. I'll tell you about it later.
PPS Summer school still stinks!!!

Suddenly, I jumped. Uncle Gary was ringing his brass bell.

"Ladies and gentlemen, start your laptops!" he said. "Summer's Cool is now in session."

I raised my hand, thinking he should probably know what happened to his brother.

"Yes, Brian?"

"I just got an e-mail from my dad. His plane crashed in Antarctica, but he's all right, and he got to ride in a cool jeep called a snowcat, and he says the South Pole telescope is amazing."

Uncle Gary shook his head. "A plane crash in the icy

wilderness at the bottom of the world—talk about dangerous! Aren't you glad you're safe with me?"

That week seemed to last forever. Every day was the same: While Aunt Jenny got an early start in her workshop, I ate breakfast with Uncle Gary, who read the news on his tablet, and Nora, who worked on her novel. Her dad didn't know what she was doing, though. Since I'd stolen the green notebook, she had written the word *homework* in big letters on the front cover and was being extra careful not to let anyone see the pages.

After breakfast, I would play soccer by myself in the backyard, pretending the shed was the goal and Uncle Gary was the goalkeeper. Imaginary Uncle Gary was terrible. I scored goal after goal while he flapped his arms like a flightless bird, unable to stop a single shot. Around the time the score reached 100 to 0, the real Uncle Gary would lean out the back door, ringing his ridiculous brass bell. School always started at eight thirty on the dot.

Once inside, my brain would go on autopilot until three forty-five when Uncle Gary would look up from his computer, say, "Well, that's another day in the books," and ring the bell again.

The constant bell ringing really got on my nerves. It wasn't like I didn't know how to read a clock. And I would have stolen the bell and buried it in the berm behind the house—but somehow I just knew Uncle Gary had a metal detector.

After school, I was free to do whatever I wanted as long as I didn't leave the yard. That's like telling someone at a buffet they can eat whatever they want as long as it's not under the sneeze guard. Boring had miles of empty sidewalks that would have been perfect for biking or skateboarding or even just walking away on. And who knows? Maybe there was even a park where kids played soccer.

There was one thing that had changed for the better since we'd been grounded: I finally had something in common with my cousin. Between classes, and before and after school, we had lots of time to talk about our adventure with Cosmo and the wasps. Nora obviously thought Cosmo was cool. Whenever I said his name, her eyes seemed to go out of focus and she would smile that weird smile again. I liked Cosmo, too, but mainly I couldn't stop thinking about exploring the Matchstick Castle. I really, really wanted to go back.

But with Uncle Gary watching us like a bionic hawk, I had no idea how we would get there. I needed to find a way to persuade Nora, the ultimate rule follower, to go. Fighting the wasps was one of the most exciting things that had ever happened to me, and the only interesting thing that had happened since I arrived. And if something else didn't happen soon, fun wasn't going to be the only thing to die in Boring—I was going to die, too.

Of boredom.

CHAPTER TEN

THE CEREBRAL CONUNDRUM

On Thursday, almost a week after our adventures with Cosmo at the Matchstick Castle, we got a lucky break. When we tried to log in to Summer's Cool, nothing happened. The laptops turned on and our browsers opened, but the Summer's Cool home page wasn't there.

Uncle Gary's screen looked even worse. It was all blue.

"Now, don't panic," said Uncle Gary, sounding like he was about to completely freak out.

He tried restarting his computer, but that didn't work. He even took the cover off the tower and looked inside with a flashlight, but, if you ask me, a chimpanzee had a better chance of fixing a car.

It was no use. Uncle Gary's computer had crashed, and he had been running the whole network off his machine.

If your teacher only exists on a computer, you can't

exactly have class without the computer. I wanted to jump up on the table and yell "Hallelujah!" before backflipping onto the carpet. Instead, I settled for a subtle fist pump and a quiet "*Yes!*" I would have high-fived Nora, but I just knew she would leave me hanging.

Uncle Gary gave me a look. "I'm sure I can get this repaired quickly. Why don't you kids come with me to Computer Shack? I think you'll find it interesting."

"We're grounded until tomorrow, remember?" said Nora.

"True enough. But I can certainly make an exception for an educational activity."

"What if we go to the library instead? That's even more educational."

Uncle Gary looked at us like we had just turned down a trip to the candy store. But what could he say? Nora was right.

"Be back by noon," he warned.

And so, while he wrapped his computer tower in a blanket and buckled it into the backseat of his minivan like a big, rectangular toddler, we got bikes out of the garage. Uncle Gary's was too big for me, so I had to ride Aunt Jenny's, which was a girl bike, but because she was a grown-up, at least it wasn't a girl-bike color.

And, anyway, I didn't care. It felt so good to be outside and whizzing down the sidewalk that I would have ridden a pink Barbie bike with purple streamers and training wheels if I had to.

I didn't have any idea where I was going, so Nora led the way. We went down curving sidewalks, across railroad tracks, and then onto a paved bike path that went behind a bunch of big chain stores. We crossed a four-lane street at a traffic light and then pedaled a few more blocks until we reached the Boring Municipal Complex, a bunch of white brick buildings that included the library, city hall, and a field house with an outdoor pool, where lots of kids were yelling and splashing.

"Why didn't you tell me there was a pool?" I asked as we pulled up at the bike rack outside the library.

"Because my dad wouldn't have agreed to that."

"You could have said 'go to the library' when you meant 'enjoy a nice swim,' you know."

Nora opened her bike chain and started threading it through the rack and both of our tires. "I don't like the chlorine. And besides, we need to look for a book."

"Does it have something to do with the book you're writing?" The chain wasn't quite long enough, so I pushed Aunt Jenny's bike closer to Nora's.

"No," she snapped, closing the lock. "As far as you're concerned, that book doesn't exist."

Inside the library, Nora obviously knew her way around. She walked right past the kids' books and up a flight of stairs to the adult section on the second floor. Fiction was filed by the authors' last names. And, as we walked down the *V* aisle, I finally figured out what she was up to.

Nora walked along the shelf, trailing her fingertips across

the spines of the books. Then she stopped and pulled out a book whose title, *The Cerebral Conundrum*, was lettered in orange.

It was by Kingsley van Dash. The cover, protected by a scratched and yellowed plastic wrapper, had a weird black-and-white geometric pattern that, when you looked at it one way, seemed to bulge outward. When you looked another way, it seemed to bulge inward.

"So it *does* exist," I observed.

"I thought the name sounded familiar," said Nora, blowing dust off the top and opening the back flap. The author's photograph showed a confident man with straight, dark hair and a short, pointy beard, wearing a shiny bathrobe with a wide black collar.

"I wonder what happened to him. Maybe he took off on an adventure like Cosmo's dad."

"Maybe."

"You know what? We should check it out and show it to your parents. If they knew that Cosmo's uncle is an author, maybe they'd want to meet him . . . although I guess someone would have to find him first. What's the book about?"

But Nora didn't answer. She was already reading.

"Can I see it?" I asked. "How old is it?"

She turned a page, ignoring me.

"Come on, Nora, at least let me read over your shoulder."

She turned away, making it impossible for me to see.

Then she sank down and sat on the floor, hunched over the book.

I sighed and went looking for comic books. They had a good selection downstairs, but I had to cut through the little kids' story time to get there. And the whole time I was browsing, I was followed by a crusty-nosed, curly-haired toddler who had wandered away from the stories. His mom was texting or something and didn't notice. I finally got the kid to stop following me by giving him a comic—he sat down, put a corner of it in his mouth, and started chewing.

When I came back at eleven thirty, Nora was still reading. She didn't argue when I told her it was time to go, but she read the book all the way to the checkout desk and then all the way to the bike rack. And when I turned around on the bike path to see why she was so far behind, I saw that she had the book open on her handlebars and was paying more attention to its pages than she was to the path ahead.

I decided to mess with her. "Look out!" I yelled.

She looked up, startled, and lost control of the bike. It was going left and she was going right, holding on to the handlebars with one hand and trying not to let go of her precious book. She only managed to avoid crashing by jumping off and letting the bike go down without her.

I circled back and waited until she had her feet on the pedals again. If I hadn't, I'm pretty sure she would have stood there reading until the sun went down.

. . .

Uncle Gary wasn't home when we got back, so Nora headed for the backyard with a glass of lemonade and *The Cerebral Conundrum* while I went downstairs to get my soccer ball. Aunt Jenny was in the laundry room but came out when she heard me.

"Laundry day, Brian!" She said it cheerfully, the way some people would say *three-day weekend*. "I need you to pick up your room and give me anything that needs to be washed."

Laundry day? I had only been there for a week and a half. At home, we did laundry once a month. My dad always said we could wear our clothes until people smelled us coming. Saving water is good for the environment, anyway.

I started picking my clothes up off the floor. I put everything that looked or smelled dirty in the hamper, and everything else back in the dresser drawers.

One pair of jeans crinkled when I picked them up. There was something stiff in the back pocket. I fished out the folded envelope from the Matchstick Castle.

I felt bad about forgetting to put the letter back—but, considering the piles of unopened letters I'd seen in Cosmo's house, it probably wouldn't have been opened even if I delivered it. Why didn't the van Dashes open their mail?

While I wondered, I folded and unfolded the envelope, then folded and unfolded it again. It looked like a flapping wing. Then, suddenly, the seal came undone. I knew that you were never, ever supposed to open anyone else's mail—but what if the envelope was already open? It obviously wasn't a personal letter.

Before I could talk myself out of it, I pulled the paper out of the envelope and started reading.

To: Dashiell van Dash
From: William White
Subject: Imminent Demolition

Dear Mr. van Dash,

As you have been heretofore and previously informed, your parcel of land (precise coordinates on file in surveyor's office) has been annexed by the City of Boring. All properties therein are therefore subject to taxation, zoning, and health safety laws and regulation of the city, not the county. Pursuant to our inspection of your property on March 15, the city finds that your property is in violation of over 177 points of municipal code, details of which have been delivered by bonded messenger on three previous occasions. In the absence of remedy to said violations, or any communication from your legal counsel in this regard, the municipality has exercised its right to condemn the property. Please be advised that this memo marks the hundredth such notification; efforts to serve notice are hereby considered exhausted. Unless compelling retort is made, demolition of property at 1 Matchstick Lane will commence at 8 a.m. on Monday,

July 11. All persons and personal property must be removed from said domicile prior to demolition.

Dutifully,
William "Bill" White
Planner, City of Boring

I read the letter again and then a third time. Some of the words were hard to understand, but the meaning was perfectly clear: The Matchstick Castle was going to be destroyed, and the van Dash family had no idea what was about to happen.

Even worse, they only had four days to stop it.

I heard the groan of the garage door over the sound of Aunt Jenny's washing machine. Uncle Gary was back. I gave my laundry to Aunt Jenny, grabbed my ball, and was running up the stairs two at a time when Uncle Gary's bell rang. I guess he'd gotten his computer fixed, because school was back in session.

CHAPTER ELEVEN

WHEN TO BREAK THE RULES

After school, I finally made it to the backyard with my soccer ball. The day was as hot and humid as ever, but now it was getting windy, making it feel like someone had opened the world's biggest oven door. Nora came out after me. She sat down under the umbrella at the patio table and took her bookmark out of *The Cerebral Conundrum*.

"Come on. Kick the ball around with me just once," I pleaded. Playing soccer alone is better than playing ping-pong alone, but just barely.

Nora rolled her eyes. "I already told you it wouldn't be any fun for you even if I did. I've never played."

"You could be a defender, at least. All you have to do is try to take the ball away when I dribble past you."

Nora looked at the book the way a lot of grown-ups look at their phones: as if they're hypnotized and helpless to resist.

"You could even just . . . stand there."

"That sounds like so much fun," she said sarcastically.

"Well, if you don't play, then I won't tell you what I learned about the Matchstick Castle."

That got her attention. She stood up, closed the book, and followed me farther into the yard.

"What did you find out?"

I pointed. "Stand over there. The shed is the goal, so you need to stop me from scoring."

"Can I use my hands?"

"Do you want to be a defender or a goalkeeper?"

"I have no idea," said Nora.

"If you're a defender, then you can use any part of your body except your shoulders, arms, and hands. If you're a goalkeeper, you can use your hands, shoulders, anything, as long as you're inside the penalty box."

"Inside a box? I thought goalkeepers played on the field like everyone else."

I sighed. "Let's just play."

Dribbling the ball, I faked left, then left again, then spun past Nora and thumped the ball against the shed to score a goal. She never even moved.

"Why didn't you try to stop me?" I asked.

"You said I could just stand here."

She had a point.

"Maybe we should just kick it to each other," I suggested.

I passed the ball to Nora's feet. She gave it a halfhearted kick, and it rolled halfway back to me before stopping.

"Nice one," I said encouragingly.

"How long do I have to do this before you tell me?"

"Until I say so. Now try again."

"Is it something about the history of the Matchstick Castle? Or did you find out where Kingsley van Dash went?"

I shook my head. "Bend your knees and use the side of your foot."

As we passed back and forth, I could see that Nora wasn't lying: She had never kicked a ball in her life. But it was better than playing by myself. And who knows? If she stuck with it and listened to me, she might go from being truly awful to just plain old bad.

"Do you have to do summer school every year?" I asked.

"This is the second year. Last year was easier because my dad was just getting started and the software was a lot simpler. But it's for my own good. If I don't get straight As in middle school, I might not get into AP classes in high school, and I need to be on the honor roll or I can forget about getting into a good college. Then my career would be as good as over."

I had never even thought about high school and college, but I did know what I wanted to be when I grew up: a professional soccer player. I couldn't imagine anything more fun than that.

"What do you want to be?" I asked.

"Well, my dad wants me to be a biomedical engineer. Either that or a market research analyst. He says there will be a lot of jobs doing those things when I'm grown up."

"I don't even know what those are," I said.

"Me neither," admitted Nora.

"But what do *you* want to be?"

This time, Nora kicked the ball really hard, and I had to go halfway across the yard to get it.

"I want to be a novelist," she said, "but my dad says you can't learn that in school."

"You can't learn everything in school."

"He also says it's practically impossible to make a living writing books."

"Well, what if you just wrote books for fun?" I said as I went running after another wild pass.

"Then what would I do for work?"

As a kid, Nora was completely hopeless. She had no idea that the real purpose of life was to *live*—to find out about the world and have adventures. If she wasn't careful, she was going to end up just like her dad. I pictured Uncle Gary with Nora's face and then shuddered, wishing I hadn't. It was just too weird.

It was time to break the bad news. I put my foot on the ball, then took the letter out of my pocket and gave it to her. While she read, she gripped the paper so hard that she practically crumpled it.

"This is horrible!" she said. "Where will they live?"

"We have to warn Cosmo," I said. "We have to deliver this letter, in person, to make sure he reads it and tells his family."

"But how? We're not supposed to go to his house."

I took a deep breath. "Listen, Nora. I know you hate breaking the rules, but there are times to follow rules, and times to break them. The Matchstick Castle is going to be *demolished*, and they have *no idea it's about to happen*."

"They should have opened their mail," she said.

"You're right."

She paused. "Even after we tell them, what happens then? According to the letter, it's already too late!"

"I don't know. But we have to warn them. It's their home. If that means breaking Uncle Gary's rules and getting grounded again, well, that's a risk I'm prepared to take," I told her. "And maybe it's time you stopped writing about adventures and had one yourself."

For a long time, Nora squinted out at the trees behind the house as if she could see all the way to the Matchstick Castle. I imagined tiny Noras arguing inside her head, one of them desperate to go help Cosmo and the other one closing her eyes, plugging her ears, and singing, "*La, la, la, I can't hear you!*"

"They invited us to dinner," I said. I couldn't think of anything else to persuade her.

She looked at me. "Wasn't that tonight?"

"Uh-huh," I said.

"Well, then, we have to go," she said matter-of-factly, like she was answering a question on a quiz. "It would be completely rude to ignore an invitation to dinner."

Who could understand the way her mind worked? That was a Cerebral Conundrum in itself.

"Well . . . great," I said. "What time should we leave?"

"Meet me in the backyard at ten forty-five—my mom and dad always go to sleep at ten thirty."

"Isn't that kind of late for dinner?"

"Uncle Montague said not to worry about when we showed up. They always eat late."

I figured we'd be lucky to get a few crumbs of dessert, but I didn't care. I was just glad we were going back to the Matchstick Castle.

CHAPTER TWELVE

THE WOODS AT NIGHT

Bedtime at Uncle Gary's was always nine o'clock sharp, whether we were tired or not.

"Sleep is important for proper physical and mental development," he said, pointing at the basement door. "If you're short on sleep, you're shortchanging yourself."

I usually fell asleep on the couch while I watched the late news with my dad, but I didn't argue. I wanted Uncle Gary to think I would be just as sound asleep as him.

Before bedtime, I searched the storage bins in my room until I found one marked CAMPING SUPPLIES. Inside, along with a gas stove, tent pegs, and nylon rope, I found some flashlights and headlamps. I picked out two headlamps, testing them to make sure the batteries worked, and closed the box again.

Then, after brushing my teeth, I put on my pajamas and

got into bed. If Uncle Gary came downstairs for some reason, I wanted everything to look normal.

I thought about setting my alarm but worried the loud beeping might wake Uncle Gary and Aunt Jenny, so I decided to stay awake for the next hour and forty-five minutes. I pulled a stack of comic books off the nightstand, fluffed my pillow, and started to read.

When I woke up, I was eyeball-to-eyeball with an alien. I jumped up. A page from a comic book, lit from behind by my reading lamp, had been lying across my face. The clock read 10:53. *Crap!*

I scrambled out of bed and almost fell over. One of my legs was asleep, so I had to walk in a circle until it woke up. My face was wet with drool, which made me wonder if the alien had licked me. I think my brain was still asleep, too.

I was panicking in slow motion. What if Nora left without me?

Grabbing my socks and shoes and the two headlamps, I opened my door slowly. It didn't make a sound. Then I crossed the cold, concrete basement floor and went upstairs to the landing. One of the steps creaked and I held my breath, but nothing happened.

I was carefully letting myself out the back door when disaster struck: The handle slipped out of my fingers and the door closed with a loud *thunk*. I froze, waiting and listening. I could see the window of Uncle Gary and Aunt Jenny's room above me. I was so sure the light would turn on that, for a second, I actually thought it did.

But the light stayed off. I crouched down to put on my socks and shoes, then straightened up to look around for my cousin.

There. I spotted Nora's silhouette on top of the berm.

Gray clouds were rushing across the dark sky. I crossed the yard and climbed over the chain-link fence as quietly as I could, but it still rattled when I let go. Rocks slid and clacked under my feet while I made my way up to her.

"I thought you were going to wake up the whole neighborhood," whispered Nora.

"Well, I didn't," I whispered back. I was tired, and that was the best I could come up with.

"Let's go before they wake up and we get grounded again."

On the far side of the berm, out of sight of the house, I finally started to breathe normally.

"I brought headlamps," I said, handing one to her.

She put it on without saying thanks and then pressed the power button. She looked like a cyclops with a glowing eye.

"Nice pajamas," she said.

In my hurry, I had forgotten to put on regular clothes.

"Well, what are you wearing?"

I turned on my headlamp and aimed it at her. She was wearing black jeans and a black long-sleeved shirt, and her hair was tied up with a dark bandanna. With a little backpack on her shoulders, she looked like a ninja spy.

"This is a secret mission, not a sleepover," said Nora.

"Fine," I said. "I'll go back and change."

"Oh, no, you won't. We're already late, and we can't risk waking up my parents. We're going. Now stop shining your light in my eyes!"

She turned and started walking. I wondered how we would find the Matchstick Castle in the dark, but Nora had planned for that. Following the berm, we walked along the outside of Sunnybright Circle—but out of sight of the houses—until we reached the path that Uncle Montague told us about.

The forest at night was as dark as a closet. There were no streetlights, obviously, and the tree branches blocked out the moon and the stars. Our headlamp beams were as bright as camera flashes, illuminating bugs, frogs, and even a pale-faced, pink-nosed little animal Nora told me was a possum. Frozen in its tracks, the possum just stared at us while we went past.

During the day, the woods had seemed quiet and sleepy, but now they were noisy and awake. Crickets chirped, cicadas whined, and bullfrogs burped while big gusts of wind shook the leaves and branches with a sound like running water. I waved away mosquitoes buzzing in my ear, my headlamp beam zigzagging across the trees. Somehow, its brightness only made the darkness seem darker.

When the path reached the gate, we turned left onto the dirt road and started walking side by side.

"How is Uncle Kingsley's book?" I asked.

"It's *amazing*," she said. "It's the best book I've ever read."

"What's it about?"

"It's . . . well, it's about a man who decides to explore his own brain."

"How does he do that? Does he shrink himself so that he can—wait, that wouldn't work, because then his brain would be smaller, too."

"No, he doesn't *shrink himself*. He does it with his mind. He's like an explorer, and there are rooms in it, and cities, and wild places, and . . . It's really hard to explain. You'd have to read it."

"Has he written any other books?" I asked.

"I don't know," said Nora. "This one was published back in 1987, so he must have written more since then. I'd love to talk to him about writing. Maybe he'd have some advice for me."

"He'll have to come back from wherever he is first. But what if he comes home, and his home isn't there anymore? What if there's nothing they can do to save the Matchstick Castle?"

"I'm sure they'll think of something."

"Really? Like what?"

"I don't know. But they're grown-ups. Grown-ups know how to solve problems."

I thought about Dashiell van Dash, Cosmo's dad, exploring the Amazon jungle and bringing back a crate full of giant deadly wasps. Then I thought about Uncle Gary and his solution for learning.

"Sometimes I think they create more problems than they solve."

The wind was getting stronger, and the clouds were moving fast. It smelled like it was going to rain.

Finally, we saw the house. Below us, in the clearing, the windows on the first two floors of the Matchstick Castle were lit up like eyes in a jack-o'-lantern.

We broke into a run: down the slope, through an opening in the crumbling wall, past the overgrown lawn furniture, and up the noisy front steps. But our racket was drowned out by something even louder: The house itself was moaning and groaning as it swayed in the wind.

We pounded our fists on the door, barely hearing our knocks over the whistling wind and creaking wood. When no one answered, I pressed my ear against the door and listened. I heard voices shouting inside. I turned the handle just as a big gust of wind pulled the doorknob out of my hand and threw the door open with a *bang*.

The shouting stopped for a second while everyone turned to stare at us. And then, right away, it all started again.

CHAPTER THIRTEEN

A MESSAGE FROM UNCLE KINGSLEY

Three red-faced men were arguing.

One of them was Uncle Montague, but I didn't recognize the other two. There was a fire burning in the fireplace—which was strange, considering how warm it was outside—and most of the smoke was coming into the room instead of going up the chimney. I heard flapping wings and looked up to see a pigeon flying in circles near the ceiling.

"Hi!" I said. "We—"

"One moment if you would, please, Brian," said Montague politely, before going back to yelling at the other two men. With all of them talking at once, I could barely understand what they were saying.

"There's no need to shout!" shouted Montague.

"If you had all listened to me—but you never listen to me!" the second man cried.

"It is a fowl, not a fish!" bellowed the third man.

"We have a very important letter for you!" I tried to yell over them, but their voices were a lot louder than mine, and they didn't hear me. *I* couldn't even hear me.

At that moment, a door opened, and Cosmo burst in carrying a net on a long pole. He looked happy to see us.

"Hi, guys! Glad you could make it," he said as he started chasing the pigeon around the room.

"We have an urgent letter—" I started to say.

"Just a minute. I have to catch this pigeon," said Cosmo.

All we could do was watch. Montague wiped his forehead with a white handkerchief, his face getting redder and redder as the shouting match continued. Cosmo wasn't able to get the pigeon, but he did net the antlers over the fireplace, the chandelier over the table, and one of the shouting men.

The smoke was making me cough. I turned to Nora.

"What should we do?"

She shrugged. "I don't think we can do anything. They're crazy."

Then a fourth man jogged down the stairs, crossed the room confidently, and jumped up on the big table. He made space to stand by kicking a stack of books out of the way.

"GENTLEMEN!" he boomed.

The men stopped arguing, Cosmo stopped running, and

suddenly the room was quiet except for the sounds of flapping wings and crackling fire.

"Arguing will get us nowhere," the man said. Then he saw us. "And it appears we have guests. Let's not forget our manners!"

He jumped down and came over, shaking our hands like he was trying to get water out of an old-fashioned pump. He was thin, with dark hair and a small mustache, and wearing tan clothes with so many pockets I wondered how he ever found his keys.

"I am Dashiell van Dash. And you are?"

"Brian Brown," I said.

"And I'm Nora Brown. We're cousins." I thought she was going to choke on the word *cousins*.

"I've heard of you! You are Cosmo's new friends. Welcome, welcome. And, Brian, allow me to compliment you on your pajamas. Simply marvelous. In the pattern, do I recognize the artwork of Giacomo Balla?"

"Um . . . they're *Star Wars*," I said, feeling myself blush.

"Ah. You have me at a disadvantage. Now, you've met my son, Cosmo, and my brother Montague. Allow me to introduce my other siblings. Captain Roald van Dash, the famed navigator, is a survivor of shipwrecks on all seven seas and several freshwater lakes. He's also the man who steered the SS *Vincible* through a typhoon on its legendary mission of mercy to Micronesia."

Roald, tall and thin with mournful eyes, red cheeks, and

a nose like a bird's beak, had a grip that seemed as damp and clammy as seawater when he shook our hands. He was wearing a thick sweater and a black stocking cap.

"How do you do?" he said, puffing on a pipe that smelled like roofing tar.

"And this is Ivar," said Dashiell, putting his hand on the shoulder of a stocky, pale man wearing old overalls and a miner's helmet with a lamp. "He is, of course, the renowned geologist, gemologist, and spelunker who discovered and mapped the crystal caves of Kam-Ranuti."

Shifting a coil of rope over his shoulder, Ivar nodded gruffly without offering to shake hands. That was fine with me. His face and hands were smudged with dirt.

"I would go on," added Dashiell, "but I'm sure you're familiar with their exploits."

From the way we were looking at him, it was probably obvious we weren't.

"A pity," said Dashiell. "But not everyone reads as much as they might."

"We have a letter for you," I said as I pulled the envelope from my pocket. I wanted to get his attention before everything got crazy again.

"How kind of you to hand deliver," said Dashiell.

"It was mailed to you, actually, but I took it with me it by accident."

Dashiell turned away without taking the letter and began pacing. "Coincidentally, a communication from our long-lost brother is why we're in a bit of an uproar here. You see, one year ago, Kingsley—the author, whose work you may well know—"

Nora nodded so fast I'm surprised she didn't get whiplash.

"—suddenly disappeared, without leaving a clue as to his whereabouts. Frankly, we'd all but given him up for lost when a message arrived via carrier pigeon."

"What does the message say?" I asked.

He held a tiny scrap of paper at arm's length and moved it slowly closer, like he was trying to bring it into focus. "It says, 'I'm all right. Hope you weren't worried. I am in . . .'"

He stopped, frowning.

"In *where*?" Nora asked.

Dashiell van Dash shook his head and tucked the note into a tiny pocket at his waist. "It doesn't say. The piece of paper is so small, he didn't have room to finish. There is a second note, on the pigeon's other leg, that may hold the answer. The bird escaped before we could read it."

Above us, the pigeon landed on the shotgun in the antlers over the fire and started grooming its feathers. Cosmo tiptoed toward it, his net ready.

"*You* let go too soon!" Roald told Ivar.

"*You* were supposed to hold the bird while *I* retrieved the note!" Ivar insisted.

Dashiell reached into his pocket, took out a cracker, and held it up in the air. He clicked his tongue to get the pigeon's attention, and it flew to him. Crumbs went everywhere as it landed on his arm and started gobbling the cracker.

"While you were all shouting," explained Dashiell, "I made a quick trip to the pantry."

He reached up and untied the note from the pigeon's other leg. He unrolled it carefully.

But the pigeon, now finished with the cracker, pinched the paper in its beak and took off. Dashiell grabbed for it and missed.

Suddenly, all of us—Montague, Ivar, Roald, Cosmo, Nora, and me—were chasing the bird. We shouted and waved our arms, making a lopsided figure eight while the freaked-out bird flew around the room, the little piece of paper dangling from its mouth like a worm. I jammed the letter from William White back into my pocket so I wouldn't lose it.

Cosmo swung the net hard and caught the pigeon—but not the note. The force of his swing knocked it out of the bird's mouth. It fluttered high above us, riding on invisible currents of air. We ran back and forth while it flew over the chandelier, hovered in a corner, and then, when a huge gust of wind outside shook the house and all the smoke was sucked back toward the chimney, flew toward the flickering fire.

"AAH!" gasped Montague, sounding as if he'd been stabbed with a fireplace poker.

We all ran over, but we were too late: The note landed right on a glowing log and started turning brown. It would catch fire any second.

Without thinking, I gave my fingers a sloppy lick and then reached into the fire and pulled it out. It was smoking but hadn't started to burn. Fortunately, my fingers weren't burning, either.

"Great work, Brian!" said Cosmo.

"Yes, great work," agreed his dad and his uncles.

"I think we can skip the high fives," said Nora, eyeing my spit-soaked hand.

"I was thinking about how you can put a candle out by pinching it if you lick your fingers first," I explained. "The saliva protects your fingers from the—"

"The note, please, Brian?" interrupted Dashiell.

"Yes, the note!" said the uncles.

I gave the singed note to Dashiell, who held it like a piece of ancient parchment. He read it and frowned.

"But what does it say?" begged Montague.

"Yes, yes, what does it say?" demanded Ivar and Roald.

The uncles all leaned forward eagerly.

Dashiell looked around at each of us before he answered. "It says that our brother Kingsley has spent the last year trapped . . . *in this very house*!"

CHAPTER FOURTEEN

COSMO'S ROOM

In the *house*?" said Uncle Montague. "But that's impossible!"

"I beg to differ, Monty," said Dashiell. "It's entirely possible. For example, when was the last time you visited the seventh floor?"

Montague shuddered. "Why, no one's been in that part of the house for years."

"But *where* in the house?" demanded Ivar.

"I don't know," said Dashiell, and he showed us why.

I had rescued most of the note, but a piece had been torn off before it even landed in the fire. The first note ended with *I am in*. The only words left on the second note were:

. . . *the house, in the room by the* . . .

"The pigeon must have swallowed part of it," said Dashiell.

"I'll kill that blasted bird!" shouted Montague. "I'll cut the note from its belly, and we'll dine on roast pigeon!"

"Come, come, my dear Monty," said Dashiell. "I don't think we'll be able to read the note after its trip down the bird's gullet. And who knows? If it's a homing pigeon, perhaps it will lead us back to Kingsley. The thing to do now is form a rescue party. Gentlemen, gather your equipment and meet me back here in half an hour!"

Dashiell, Montague, Ivar, and Roald all hurried off in different directions. Cosmo freed the pigeon from the net and, holding its wings, rubbed its head with his finger.

"I wonder if my father's right," he said. "What if it can lead us to Uncle Kingsley?"

He tossed the pigeon into the air. We watched hopefully while it flapped its wings, soared toward the grand staircase—and landed on the railing, where it started cleaning its feathers again. If this dumb bird helped anyone find anything, it was going to be completely by accident.

"Well, it was worth a try," said Cosmo. "I'll take you back to my room. I need some supplies for the expedition."

I still thought we should have tried Montague's suggestion for getting the note out of the bird.

We followed Cosmo up the stairs and halfway down a narrow hall, where he stopped in front of a big wooden cabinet.

"Secret entrance," he explained, opening one of the doors and crawling inside.

We followed him and came out in a different hall, with a ceiling so short we had to duck our heads. Cosmo went so fast that we soon lost sight of him. Did he ever slow down?

I was hurrying to catch up, so I didn't notice when there suddenly wasn't a floor in front of me anymore. I teetered on the edge of a forty-foot drop, windmilling my arms.

Nora grabbed my pajamas from behind, and I caught my balance.

"Thanks. You probably saved my life," I told her.

She looked at me like she wasn't sure if I was being sincere. "You're welcome."

Meanwhile, Cosmo was circling the room on a rickety wooden catwalk that lined the walls, jumping from plank to plank.

"This is his *room*?" I said. I felt dizzy just looking at it.

"He must be very brave," said Nora. "Or else not very well rested. I wouldn't be able to sleep for a second."

It wasn't like any bedroom I'd ever seen. It was three or four stories tall and looked like someone had put a handful of rooms in a blender, and the different parts were stuck to the sides of the jar. There were balconies and windows and doors up and down the walls, but there were walls behind some of the windows, and some of the doors didn't have stairs leading up to them. There were bookshelves so high that no one could have reached them from the floor and chairs on the wall that no one could have gotten down from. And the only way you could tell someone even slept there was the three hammocks hanging from the middle of the ceiling, high above the floor.

Like a sailor on an old wooden ship, Cosmo grabbed hold of a rope, pushed off a plank, and swung out into the middle of the room, where he climbed into a hammock like a monkey.

"Come on!" he called. "There's plenty of room for you both!"

Nora was still holding tight to the back of my pajamas. I shook her off and then, after taking a deep breath, stepped onto the nearest plank. The wood creaked a warning.

"Come on, Nora," I said, not a hundred percent sure I wanted to go either.

Nora shook her head and sat down. "Someone will have to tell my parents what happened to you after you plunge to your death. It might as well be me."

I kept going, doing my best to do everything the same way Cosmo did. It took me twice as long, and I had to make a few swings on the rope before I felt confident enough to grab one of the empty hammocks, but I finally made it.

Cosmo was busy filling his pockets with things from his pillowcase: a pocketknife, a compass, a cool pair of folding binoculars, a box of matches, and a whistle. He looked completely relaxed in his swaying hammock, but I couldn't stop thinking about how high up we were. I didn't even want to look over the edge in case I accidentally flipped over—I would have ended up as flat as a fried egg. They would have needed a spatula to get me off the floor.

When Cosmo had all the things he needed, he looked over and saw Nora still sitting at the edge of the room, a safe distance from the drop.

"What are you doing over there, Nora? Come join us!" he called cheerfully.

"Thank you, but I'd rather not."

"You're not scared, are you?"

"Maybe a little," she admitted.

Right away, Cosmo jumped out of his hammock, swung across the room, and went back along the catwalk to where she was. With lots of encouragement and a little actual hand-holding, he brought her to the rope and then swung across with her on it.

By the time Nora climbed into the third hammock, her face was pink with excitement.

"See? Nothing to be afraid of," said Cosmo.

"Fear of falling is perfectly rational," said Nora, still breathing hard. "But why do you have three hammocks?"

"For sleepovers. I mean, I haven't had any, but you never know."

"If you lived anywhere else, I know you'd have lots of friends."

She was right. If Cosmo went to my school, he would have been one of the coolest kids there. But being the only kid living with so many grown-ups made him act a little bit grown-up, too. In that way, I guess he was similar to Nora—maybe that was why she liked him so much.

I decided to change the subject before they started gazing deep into each other's eyes. "I can't believe your uncle got lost in his own house."

"Uncle Kingsley isn't an explorer or an adventurer in the same way as my father and my other uncles," said Cosmo. "As an author, he explores his own mind. He calls it"—he paused and lowered his voice, like he was imitating his uncle—"'braving the depths of that most frightening place: the human brain.' Ever since I can remember, he's been taking his typewriter and going off to write somewhere new. The house inspires him, so he writes different kinds of things in different rooms. 'Every room in this house has a story,' he says."

Hanging in the middle of Cosmo's bedroom, it was easy to imagine that some of the rooms had more than one story.

"That sounds just like his book *The Cerebral Conundrum*," said Nora, leaning forward but holding tight to her hammock. "I'm reading it, you know."

"You are? That's my favorite one!" he said.

"How many more has he written?" asked Nora.

"Twenty-seven."

"But our library only has the one."

"Oh, none of the others have been published."

"But didn't you say he was famous?" I asked.

Cosmo leaned back and folded his arms behind his head. "Well, he should be. It usually takes him about a year and a half to write a new one, and when he's done, we always have a big party to celebrate. Uncle Montague makes more food than you can possibly imagine—breakfasts, lunches, and dinners—so we have plenty to eat while we listen to Uncle Kingsley read it out loud."

"All of it?" I asked, imagining sitting still for a whole novel.

Cosmo nodded. "Sometimes it takes three or four days. When Uncle Kingsley's finally done, he makes a few more changes and then mails the manuscript to his agent in New York, who sends the book out to publishers. Most of the mail is for Uncle Kingsley—and it's usually rejection letters, unfortunately."

While he was talking, Nora tried to copy him by lying down in her hammock, but the moment she felt it start to sway, she panicked and sat up again. "Doesn't he get discouraged?"

"Of course! But van Dashes aren't quitters. Our family motto is 'Do great things and let others watch.' Unfortunately, people aren't watching as much as they used to. Someday, though, the world will recognize his genius."

"And he's been missing for a whole year?" I asked.

Cosmo nodded. "One morning, he went off to write as usual and just never came back. Unfortunately, it was days before anyone noticed. There's usually a lot going on here."

"Didn't you search the house?"

"Well, most of it. But no one had ever been lost in the house before, so we didn't really think that was the problem.

We thought he had probably gotten caught up in an adventure by accident or maybe kidnapped by gypsies. Uncle Montague says gypsies love a good storyteller."

"So you haven't been opening the mail?" asked Nora.

"I guess we haven't," said Cosmo.

"Brian, show him."

I took the letter out of my pocket and unfolded it. By now, it was so beat up that it looked a year old.

"Cosmo, the Matchstick Castle really is in danger."

"What's that?"

"Something you have to read."

Unfortunately, our hammocks were too far apart and I couldn't hand him the letter. And if either of us reached any farther, we were going to have a very short flying lesson—which gave me an idea. I folded the letter into a paper plane and sailed it over.

Cosmo caught it easily and unfolded it. Nora and I didn't say anything while he read, frowning. Finally, he looked up.

"This William White can't be serious, can he?"

"He certainly sounds serious," said Nora.

"We need to show this to your dad and your uncles," I told Cosmo.

"We'll do it the moment we find Uncle Kingsley," he agreed.

"Shouldn't we do it right away? There's only Friday, Saturday, and Sunday left before they demolish your house!"

"And that's exactly why we can't distract them: We have

to get Kingsley out before it happens. Speaking of which, we should get back. They'll be ready by now."

I peered over the side of my hammock. Somehow, the return trip seemed trickier. Nora looked even more nervous than I felt.

"Aren't you ever afraid you'll fall out of bed?" she asked him.

"I did, once," said Cosmo. "But when I woke up I was holding onto the rope. I had been dreaming about wrestling a snake."

Cosmo handed Nora the rope and made sure she was holding on tight before he pushed off. He pumped his legs, and they swung back and forth, going a little bit farther each time. When they were close enough—but not as close as I would have wanted to be—they let go, flew through the air, and landed on a plank that bounced up and down under their weight.

"Wow!" said Nora, pushing her hair out of her eyes.

"Your turn, Brian!" called Cosmo.

Catching the rope in both hands as it swung toward me, I pushed off from the hammock. But I didn't swing back and forth like Cosmo and Nora did—I just dangled. I pumped my legs, but I couldn't seem to get moving.

"Help!" I said.

"There's nothing I can do—I can't reach you," said Cosmo. "Pump your legs more."

"I'm trying!"

My hands and arms were getting tired. I didn't know how long I could hold on.

"I was afraid this would happen," said Nora, completely ignoring the fact that she had Cosmo's help the whole way.

"Well, you can always just climb down the rope," said Cosmo.

Besides falling, there wasn't anything else I *could* do. I started wriggling downward, squeezing the rope between my feet to take some of the weight off my hands.

Looking up, I saw Cosmo and Nora watching me. They were a long way up. And the farther down I went, the darker it got.

"What do I do when I get to the bottom?" I called.

"That's easy. Take the middle door and go left, then right, then down the hall to the dead end. Open the secret door, climb the stairs, and we'll meet you there."

I repeated the directions in my mind so I wouldn't forget them. Middle door . . . left . . . right . . . down the hall to the dead end. Open the secret door—*secret door*?

"Cosmo!" I shouted. "How do I find the secret door?"

But they were already gone.

Making things even worse, I was out of rope. My feet dangled in the air, and my fingers were losing their grip. It was so dark at the bottom of the tall room that I had no idea how far I had left to fall.

For once I wondered if Uncle Gary had the right idea about how dangerous the Matchstick Castle was. But I sure didn't want him to be right. I didn't want to break any bones when I hit the floor, either.

Closing my eyes, I bent my legs and let go.

CHAPTER FIFTEEN

THE RESCUE PARTY

Almost as soon as I let go, I landed.

I didn't go splat. My legs weren't broken and my ankles weren't sprained. I didn't even fall over.

It was so dark in the lower part of Cosmo's room that, while I was holding on to the rope, I didn't realize I had almost reached the floor. I think I only dropped about three feet.

As my heartbeat returned to normal, my eyes adjusted to the darkness. Dirty clothes, comic books, toys, and balls were scattered all over the floor. It wasn't that different from my room back home, I realized. Neither of us had moms around to make us clean up after ourselves. And our dads weren't like Uncle Gary.

I didn't want to get left behind and miss the rescue party, so I looked for the way out. I found the middle door without any problem because there were only three to choose from. When I turned the doorknob and pulled, though, it came off in my hand.

I tried to put it back on, but there wasn't any way to do it. I tried opening the door with my fingertips—and even my fingernails—but it wouldn't budge. The thing was shut tight.

Remembering that the next part of Cosmo's directions was to turn left, I tried the door on the left. It opened just fine, but there was a wall behind it. Apparently, it was just a decorative door.

The door on the right was my only hope of getting out. I didn't think I was strong enough to climb back up the rope. And even if I could, I'd never be able to swing over to the catwalk.

I turned the knob and pulled.

The door opened. No wall.

I was out! Anxious to catch up with everyone else, I headed down a hall lit by tiny, old-fashioned lightbulbs. Cosmo's directions for the middle door probably wouldn't work for this one, so I figured the best thing to do was keep moving. The hall seemed to go on and on until it disappeared into infinity.

There were lots of doors off the hallway, and I opened each one, thinking I might run out of hallway before I found an exit. Behind the first door was a stone staircase that led down into a cellar, where old barrels were stacked to the ceiling. Behind the second door, on the opposite side of the hall, was a little room filled with tiny, fluffy, white feathers—I had no idea how deep they were. The third door was locked.

The hallway kept shrinking as I went along: The ceiling got lower, the floor slanted up, and the walls got closer together. The infinite hallway was just an optical illusion, I realized. The doors got smaller, too, and by the time I was halfway to the end, the doors were barely as wide as I was. When I opened one of them, I saw a car that looked like it was a hundred years old in a room that was barely bigger than the car itself. How did they get it in there?

More importantly, *why*?

By now, the ceiling was so low that I had to crawl and the doors were so small that all I could do was look through them, at rooms that were so full of things—old stoves and pots and pans, gears and machinery, stacks of yellowed newspapers—that I couldn't imagine how or why or when they might be needed.

When I couldn't go any farther, I realized I could hear noise above me: footsteps and lots of voices, all talking at the same time.

"I'm down here!" I yelled. "How do I get out?"

It got quiet for a second. Someone said something, and then I heard scrapes and thumps like they'd suddenly decided to rearrange the furniture.

I pounded on the ceiling, and it moved a little. I pushed hard, and a square piece of it went up and fell over backward with a loud bang.

A trapdoor! I climbed up out of the tiny hallway and found myself in the great hall, with everyone looking down at me and the long table pushed to one side.

"About time," said Nora.

Cosmo didn't want me to distract the grown-ups with bad news, but it didn't seem right not to tell them—especially when they only had three days before the demolition started.

"Cosmo, show them the letter," I said.

Reluctantly, he took it out of his pocket.

"Why, it looks like a paper airplane," said Dashiell.

"It is, but—"

"It must be *airmail*," interrupted Uncle Montague. The two of them started laughing.

"Speaking of good laughs, did you see the old car downstairs?" asked Dashiell. "One of Montague's famous pranks."

Instead of answering, I took the letter from Cosmo and pushed it into Dashiell's hand. "Please read it."

"I'll do it the moment we find Kingsley. Time for assignments!"

The hall was piled with rescue equipment, and the grown-ups were all dressed for the search. Uncle Ivar was still wearing his miner's helmet, but now he had so many coils of rope over his shoulders that it looked like someone had used him as a giant spool. He also had a big backpack with a pickax, a lantern, and a bundle of dynamite hanging off it.

"Ivar, you take the basement," said Dashiell.

"Obviously," said Ivar as he opened the door to go downstairs.

Uncle Roald was wearing a yellow raincoat and a yellow rain hat. He carried a polished brass gizmo with gears and lenses.

"You won't be needing your sou'wester and your sextant tonight, Roald," said Dashiell. "I want you to search floors three and four."

Uncle Roald was obviously disappointed. He took off his raincoat as he headed for the staircase.

Uncle Montague was wearing an apron and had a flashlight and a giant walkie-talkie with an antenna that must have been a yard long.

"Monty, you take the first and second floors."

"On my way!" said Uncle Montague. He clicked his heels together, saluted, and jogged off.

Only Dashiell was left—and us kids, of course.

"I'm going to search the fifth and sixth floors," he told us. "And I'm leaving the most important job for you: the seventh floor."

When Cosmo heard the word *seventh*, he stopped smiling—it was the first time I ever saw him do that.

"The seventh floor?" he asked. "Are you sure?"

Dashiell crouched down and put his hand on Cosmo's shoulder. "It's dangerous, but I know you can do it. I have complete faith in all of you."

"But . . . *why?*" asked Nora.

I wondered that, too. After all, he barely even knew us.

Dashiell van Dash hung coils of rope around our necks like he was giving us medals for bravery. "Children can do much more than grown-ups give them credit for. Just because you're smaller than us, it doesn't mean you can't be clever, brave, and resourceful."

After hearing that, I would have been ready to tap-dance on the roof if he'd told us to. Dashiell kept loading us: extra flashlights, canteens of water, brown-bag lunches, a compass, and a flare gun. I would have felt prepared for anything if I wasn't still wearing my pajamas.

"You're also lighter than us," continued the great explorer. "The top of the house is unstable and its wood is rotten. Adults are liable to fall right through the floorboards. But you weigh less, so you won't. Probably. Now hurry—there's no time to waste!"

As he disappeared up the stairs, there was a pure white flash of lightning outside followed by a crack of thunder that sounded like a starting gun.

"Let's go," said Cosmo.

He opened the door that Ivar had gone through and started down the steps. Nora and I followed, but not before I noticed that Dashiell had left the letter behind on the table.

"If we're supposed to search the seventh floor, why are we going downstairs?" asked Nora.

"You can get all the way to the sixth floor from the front of the house, but the front stairway to the seventh floor collapsed three years ago," Cosmo explained. "Now the only way to get there is to go down through the cellar to the back of the house and then make our way up through the servants' quarters."

"You have servants?" I asked.

"No," said Cosmo. "Do you?"

"I wish," I told him.

We went down and down until the light behind us disappeared. It smelled like we were going into a cave. At the bottom of the stairs was a dirt floor with tunnels leading off in different directions under low brick arches. Cosmo led the way, using his flashlight to warn us away from things like jagged iron bars and holes in the floor.

We passed one dark doorway where a cold breeze gave us goose bumps and another one where the air coming out was warm and dry. Then, ahead of us, a red flame sparked and sizzled. We got closer and saw Uncle Ivar lighting a cigar with a smoking, spitting road flare. He was sitting on the ground, dangling his legs in a deep, dark hole. One end of a rope was tied to a wooden beam above the hole and the other end was tied around his waist.

"Where does that lead?" I asked.

"All sorts of places," said Uncle Ivar. "I know these holes better than anybody, and I still don't know half of 'em."

Puffing on his cigar, Uncle Ivar dropped the flare. The tunnel got darker. I leaned forward and watched the red flame spin as it fell down the shaft, landing silently far below.

"Well, that's me, then," said Uncle Ivar.

Grabbing the rope and looping it under his butt, he pushed off with his legs and started rappelling down the wall of the shaft. Soon all we could see of him was the glowing red tip of his cigar.

"Good luck, Uncle Ivar!" called Cosmo.

His voice echoed: ". . . *Uncle Ivar . . . Uncle Ivar . . . Uncle Ivar . . .*"

Cosmo led us farther down the tunnel and through a small metal hatch in the wall. Behind the hatch was a big room—or was it a cave?—where the floor was hilly and covered with white mushrooms. We jumped across a small stream in the middle of the room, then climbed uphill to a door and went through into a dusty hallway lined with sooty wooden bins. At the end of that hall, a wooden ladder was nailed to the wall. Cosmo climbed up it like a spider and disappeared through a square hole in the ceiling. We went up after him into a tall, narrow hallway.

"Now we're on the first floor again," said Cosmo.

He used a long match to light a gas lamp, and we saw that the walls were lined with cupboards, shelves, and what looked like little wooden mailboxes. There was a big board where small circles were labeled with at least a hundred room names, a brass switchboard, and even, as he showed us, a pneumatic tube with a message cylinder resting in the basket below it.

"Why doesn't your uncle Kingsley just ring the buzzer or use the message tube?" I asked, thinking those would have worked a lot better than the pigeon.

"The message systems were never connected," said Cosmo. "And there never were any servants, but it wasn't for lack of planning by my great-grandfather. The house is so big that efficient communication would have been essential."

"What did your great-grandfather do?" I asked.

"What *didn't* he do? That's what I'd like to know."

He pointed to a narrow, crooked flight of stairs.

"That's the way up."

"I still don't know why the kids got the most dangerous job," said Nora. "That doesn't sound fair at all."

"Well," said Cosmo. "It may not be fair, but it is logical. And no one's ever actually fallen through the floorboards yet—at least, not that I know of. I guess that could be what happened to Kingsley."

"How reassuring," said Nora.

CHAPTER SIXTEEN

SECRETS OF THE MATCHSTICK CASTLE

Walking single file, we followed Cosmo up the flight of creaking stairs. We went through a hallway lined with tiny bedrooms and a room filled with little round tables and big comfy armchairs and then went up again. The walls in this stairwell were so close together, they practically touched our shoulders.

"If the top of the house is a death trap, why would your uncle Kingsley go up there?" I asked.

"Maybe he was searching for inspiration," suggested Nora.

"He might not be there, but we have to look," said

Cosmo. “He is the smallest of my uncles, and it’s possible the floorboards could support him.”

He disappeared around a corner, and we hurried to catch up. I think both Nora and I were a little afraid of getting lost like Uncle Kingsley. The stairs didn’t go back and forth with regular turns but were completely unpredictable, turning left and then right before curving in a circle. On every landing, hallways led off into darkness and who knows where.

The steps were all different sizes, too, something Nora found out when she tripped and fell on a tall one.

“Cosmo!” she yelped.

“Yes?” he asked, appearing in front of her so quickly that he scared her and she yelped again.

“Can you go a little slower?” she asked.

Cosmo helped her to her feet. “I’ll try.”

We went higher, and the storm got louder. Thunder boomed, wind howled, and rain lashed against the windowpanes. The whole house moved from side to side like a ship on the ocean, which reminded me of a question I’d been wanting to ask.

“Cosmo!” I yelled, using the handrail to pull myself up some steps that were about two feet tall. “Why is there a boat on your roof?”

“In case of floods,” he answered over his shoulder as if it were the most natural thing in the world.

Maybe I was just tired, or maybe I’d already seen so many

weird things tonight that nothing would have surprised me. Or maybe the storm was so strong that it was easy to imagine a flood deep enough to drown the tallest house in Illinois. But it kind of made sense.

We were only climbing seven stories—eight if you counted the basement—but it felt like a hundred. The bigger- and smaller-sized steps, the dizzy back-and-forth turns, and the swaying of the house made it really hard work.

Then, when my legs were so tired I could barely lift them, Cosmo led us away from the stairs, down a long, zigzag hallway, and through a set of double doors.

"The grand ballroom!" he said proudly, drawing the words out like a radio announcer.

When it was new, it really must have been something. There were paintings in fancy frames and glass chandeliers hanging from the ceiling. A balcony looked down onto the room, and I could imagine Dashiell, Montague, Ivar, and Roald as kids, sneaking out of bed and spying on their parents' parties. It would have been a perfect place for butlers to serve food and drinks to people in fancy clothes—if they'd ever had servants.

Maybe they'd never had parties, either. Now the dance floor was splintered, the paintings were torn, and the chandeliers were covered with dust. The stormy sky showed through big holes in the corners of the ceiling. The rain was making puddles on the floor.

"Is this the seventh floor?" asked Nora.

Cosmo shook his head. "The sixth. I thought we should eat something first."

Taking off his pack, he spread out a blanket in the middle of the room. He put sandwiches, apples, and bottles of lemonade on the blanket.

It was a weird time to stop for a picnic. Kingsley was waiting to be rescued, and so was the Matchstick Castle. It gave me a sick feeling to think what would happen if we couldn't find Kingsley before the house got demolished.

On the other hand, I was starving. I grabbed a sandwich, took a big bite—and realized I had a mouthful of liverwurst. It tasted like dog food, but I chewed, swallowed, and took another bite, anyway.

"Pickled okra?" asked Cosmo, holding out a jar of something that looked like the eggs of a giant alien insect.

I decided I'd stick with the dog food.

We sat there eating on a dance floor that almost seemed to be dancing itself. The Matchstick Castle was never quiet, but in here it sounded like an orchestra going full blast. Timbers groaned like strings, and thunder boomed like drums. Wind howled through the holes in the walls like horns and woodwinds. Once I even heard breaking glass, like a crashing cymbal.

"So your great-grandfather built this house?" I shouted.

Cosmo nodded and raised his own voice. "His name was Angus Archibald McCulloch van Dash. He was very poor, so he left his sweetheart in the old country and sailed to

America to make his fortune. Unfortunately, he wasn't very good at making money. He thought he could get rich doing things nobody had ever done before, but it turned out there was a reason no one had ever done them."

"Like what?" asked Nora, nibbling around the edges of her sandwich like she was trying to avoid what was inside.

"Well, he tried to milk aphids, for one thing. He also tried to get farmers to buy painted portraits of their crops. And he tried to domesticate mice. But aphid milk only tastes good to ants, the farmers weren't interested in pictures of their corn, and, even though he was able to train the mice to do small chores, they didn't do enough work to make it worth the trouble."

"He doesn't sound very successful." I finished my sandwich and grabbed an apple. I should have guessed it would be tart, not sweet.

"He was a *financial* failure," Cosmo corrected me. "Which isn't the same thing as a *failure* failure. But then he got really lucky. He bought this land for cheap from a miner who said there were no precious minerals left. And nobody else wanted land that was so full of tunnels. When great-grandfather Archie started to dig foundations for his house, he broke into an old mine shaft, where he found a chest full of Confederate gold. And that's how he became rich!"

"How rich?" asked Nora.

"As rich as a king, but of a really small country. Right

away he sent his sweetheart a letter, but she must not have believed him about the gold. So he decided to build the biggest, best, most amazing house in the United States, a house that would take care of us as long as we took care of it. If she saw a picture of *that*, he thought, she would definitely change her mind. So he kept building."

"I guess he wasn't any better at building than he was at business," said Nora.

"Why would you say that?" he asked.

"Well, who would put a ballroom on the sixth floor of a house with no elevator?"

"He probably should have made some blueprints before he started, it's true," Cosmo admitted.

"And the stairs are crooked," Nora continued, "the doors and windows are all the wrong size, and you never know if you're going to find a deadly pit behind an ordinary-looking door!"

Cosmo frowned. "Don't you *like* the Matchstick Castle?"

"*I* do!" I said. "I wish I lived here. I could have adventures every day without even leaving home."

I had finished the apple and was still so hungry that I decided to try a piece of pickled okra. It tasted even uglier than it looked.

"I didn't mean that I don't like it," said Nora, backpedaling. "It just takes a little getting used to. Especially when you've always lived in a normal house. But it's definitely . . . very . . . creative."

Cosmo cheered up. "It *is* creative, isn't it? Like a painting, or a story, or a puzzle, or a maze. Anyway, my great-grandfather built and built and built and sent his sweetheart paintings, photographs, and even a model of the house made out of actual matchsticks. But she still wouldn't come. She said she liked her little cottage better and she was afraid she would get lost in such a big house. I guess she was a little bit like you, Nora."

For some reason, that made her cheeks turn as red as the apples. I spit my sour, slimy mouthful of okra into a napkin.

Cosmo started packing up the picnic.

"But if your great-grandmother never came to America," said Nora, wrapping her uneaten sandwich in wax paper, "how did your great-grandfather start a family?"

"He went back to the old country and married her. He was afraid someone might steal the gold on the way over, so he hid it in an old tunnel before he left. They had one son, who married and went on to have five sons of his own: Montague, Kingsley, Roald, Ivar, and Dashiell. But the little cottage they were living in was really crowded. With five growing grandsons, my great-grandmother finally admitted they all could use a bigger house, so they sailed to America. My father and his brothers grew up here."

"Do you have any brothers or sisters or cousins?" I asked as we all stood up.

Cosmo shook his head.

"What about your mother?" asked Nora. "What happened to her?"

"She's a daredevil and an aviatrix," said Cosmo proudly. "She's circumnavigating the globe in a replica of Amelia Earhart's famous Lockheed Electra 10E."

"How long has she been gone?" Nora asked.

"Oh, she left just before Uncle Kingsley disappeared."

The way he said it, she could have gone to the grocery store. I didn't know how he could be so calm about it.

Nora looked worried. "Shouldn't she be back by now?"

"She crashed," said Cosmo. "Uncle Montague received a relayed radio message right before she went down. If anyone can survive in the jungles of Borneo, though, it's my mom."

Slowly, we started crossing the ballroom floor toward the big double doors.

I could tell Nora was confused, something she wasn't used to. When you think you know everything, you don't get a lot of practice at it.

"But why haven't we heard all about your mom on the news? And your dad and your uncles? Your family should all be famous!"

"We used to be. My dad says there were reporters hanging around all the time when he was growing up—his dad was an adventurer, too. But then the *Boring News* went out of business, and I guess people got more interested in watching celebrities on TV than reading about exploration and things."

"You could be on TV, too," said Nora. "You could have your own show."

"Why don't you use the internet to tell everybody about your adventures?" I asked.

"My dad won't buy a computer. He says using them doesn't count as doing anything. And he says TV takes the mystery out of things."

We stopped in front of the doors. "Can he tell that to my uncle Gary? He thinks nothing counts *unless* you do it on a computer."

"I think my dad is actually a little bit afraid of computers, which is kind of funny for a guy who swam down the River of No Return. I guess he wishes it was more like the old days. He says a lot of famous people today have no idea how to dig a snow cave or navigate by the stars."

"Maybe those things aren't as important as they used to be," said Nora.

"Those things will always be important," said Cosmo confidently.

A flash of lightning filled the windows, followed by a roll of thunder so loud that it was like being trapped inside a kettledrum. Cosmo opened the doors.

"Why didn't your grandfather finish the house?" I asked, thinking about the gold and wondering how many millions, or even billions, it would be worth in modern times. Probably enough to build a real castle.

"He couldn't afford to," answered Cosmo. "He hid the

chest of gold so well, and was gone so long, he couldn't find it when he got back. Uncle Ivar spends most of his time looking for it down in the tunnels. We could definitely use the money to fix some things. The doorbell, for example."

"If you need help with the to-do list, just let me know," said Nora.

Cosmo smiled and headed for the door. "It'll turn up one of these days. Now let's see if Uncle Kingsley is upstairs!"

CHAPTER SEVENTEEN

THE SEVENTH FLOOR

We ran up a staircase where the steps were so short and close together that it felt like we were tap-dancing. At the top of the stairs, a door was swinging in the wind. Cosmo opened it, and we followed him cautiously onto the seventh floor.

I didn't feel ready to trust the hallway with my full weight, so I tested the wooden floorboards by stamping lightly with my foot. There was a long, low creak.

"Brian?" said Cosmo.

The creak kept going, getting louder and lower, like a giant was bending a pine tree between two hands.

"Yeah?" I said, which was hard to do because I was holding my breath.

Then there was a deafening *CRACK*, and Nora shrieked as the floor beneath us suddenly dropped a couple of inches.

We froze, wondering if we were about to go crashing down to the basement.

"Please walk very lightly."

The floor stopped moving. Barely daring to breathe, we tiptoed over to a place where it hadn't sunk.

"This is crazy," murmured Nora, like she was afraid that using her regular voice would make the house fall down.

The lights didn't work, so we turned on our headlamps and flashlights. The seventh floor looked like the rest of the house, only even more random: The ceilings were all different heights, the doorways looked like trapezoids and parallelograms, and all the windows looked into other rooms instead of outside. There was a new sound, too, with lots of scurrying and clicking little feet moving up and down inside the walls.

"Are those . . . rats?" asked Nora with a shudder.

Cosmo shook his head. "Only squirrels."

"So you've been up here before?" I asked.

"Sure," said Cosmo. "Well . . . once . . . a long time ago."

He said we should split up so we could search faster, but Nora wanted to follow Cosmo and I kind of did, too. We shined our lights where he shined his and walked so close behind him that, when he stopped, we all bumped into each other.

"We have to spread out," he warned. "If we stand too close, we'll be as heavy as Uncle Montague!"

We all tiptoed a few steps away from each other.

Walking as if we were on ice, we searched hall by tilting

hall and room by odd-shaped room. Some of the rooms had roots coming down through the ceiling, like weeds had sprouted on the roof and then grown down into the house, but others seemed warm and dry. We found one that was piled with rusty chains and another one that was filled with old sea chests.

A swaying rope ladder hung in the middle of one hallway.

"That must lead to the boat," said Cosmo.

"Could your uncle Kingsley be up there?" I asked.

"I guess it's possible."

"Your father didn't say anything about searching *above* the seventh floor," said Nora, shrinking away from the ladder.

"He also didn't tell us not to. And since nobody else is up here, we're the only ones who can do it—so we'd better look."

Holding his flashlight in his teeth like a pirate holding a knife, Cosmo climbed up the ancient-looking rope ladder and disappeared through the ceiling.

I put my hands on the ladder, ready to follow him.

"We should wait here," said Nora nervously. "That's the only sensible thing to do. In this storm, that boat might blow right off the roof."

"It's been there for a long time, and it hasn't blown off yet," I pointed out.

"What if it's gotten an inch closer to the edge every time the wind blows, and this is the night it finally goes over—do you think Cosmo will be all right?"

"Let's find out."

Nora wrung her hands and moved closer. "What if Uncle Kingsley really is up there? And what if whatever happened to him also happens to Cosmo? They might need our help!"

"It's possible," I told her, getting ready to climb.

Suddenly, Nora pushed me out of the way and started pulling herself up the ladder.

"Well, since you asked so nicely, go ahead!" I called after her.

Did she have a crush on Cosmo or what? Shaking my head, I followed her through the ceiling. It was dark, I couldn't see anything, and Nora was making the rope swing around so much that I could hardly get my feet in the rungs. Then I felt a cool breeze and a splash of water and my head popped out into the storm. The boat towered above me, resting on a huge wooden frame that lifted it above the pointy roof. The rope ladder went up the mossy, weedy shingles, up the side of the boat, and past the painted name SS *Vincible*. Wiping the rain out of my eyes, I saw Nora climb over the rail of the boat and disappear.

I scrambled onto the slick roof. The wind made my pajamas flap like a flag, and the rain practically blinded me. Holding on to the rope with a death grip, I suddenly remembered the time I'd tried waterskiing and swallowed most of Lake George. I sure hoped this would end better than that.

I pulled myself hand over hand until I fell onto the deck of the boat. Nora was on all fours next to me, looking seasick.

Cosmo grinned at us, perfectly relaxed on his own two feet.

"Nice climbing, you two! Let's search the *Vincible*. I'll take belowdecks, and you search the upper deck and the pilot house."

Calling his uncle's name, Cosmo opened a hatch and disappeared.

I stood up and grabbed the railing. Flashes of lightning made the night as bright as day, with fat raindrops looking white and frozen while the forest shook in the wind like a raging ocean. When the thunder boomed and it got dark again, I could see the streetlights of Boring in the distance. Just a few miles away, normal people were sleeping in their normal houses. I wondered if any of them were dreaming anything half as exciting as what we were actually doing.

Closer, just on the other side of the forest, I could see the houses lining Sunnybright Circle. I tried to pick out Uncle Gary's, but it was impossible. From here, all the houses looked exactly the same.

The height made me feel dizzy. The way the deck was moving, like the *Vincible* was really riding waves, I wondered if Nora was right and we were one big gust away from sailing off into a watery grave.

There wasn't much to search. After I circled halfway around the deck, I met up with Nora, who was clinging to a railing. She hadn't seen the lost writer, either. I opened the door to the pilot house, and Nora hurried in after me.

It was dry inside, but the rain splashing the windows reminded me of a car wash. The ship's wheel spun right and then left as the wind blew the rudder from side to side. Uncle Roald kept the pilot house tidy: The brass was shiny and everything was neatly put away, except for a map of the river that ran behind the Matchstick Castle and through the middle of Boring.

Nora stood up, holding on to the map table with both hands.

"If this is Uncle Roald's boat, where do you think he sailed it?" I asked. "And how did he get it up here?"

"I think the real question is *why* did he get it up here?" asked Nora.

"Cosmo said it was in case of floods."

Right when I said his name, Cosmo came in, letting the wind slam the door behind him.

"Uncle Kingsley's not in the cabins, the mess hall, the galley, the hold, or the engine room."

"Well, he's not up here, either," I said. "Did he come up here very often?"

Cosmo shook his head. "I don't think so. He's always been afraid of water."

"Seems like someone who's afraid of water would also be afraid of boats."

"Come to think of it, he hasn't written any stories with boats in them," said Cosmo. "He's probably downstairs."

I groaned.

"I don't see how having the SS *Vincible* on the roof will help in a flood," said Nora.

"The next five-hundred-year flood should crest at about this height. It's been five hundred nine years since the last one, so it's nearly ten years late. Uncle Roald generously offered the *Vincible* as our lifeboat."

"But how did he get it up here?" I asked.

Cosmo looked at me like the answer was obvious. "Well, he's a master seaman, so he's very good with a block and tackle, and ropes and knots."

"Doesn't he miss having his boat in the water?"

"Well, he spends more time piloting our sub—Listen, Brian. Uncle Roald is safe and sound. It's Uncle Kingsley who needs our help. This can wait."

He was right. We climbed down the ladder, which was a lot harder than climbing up, until we reached the seventh floor. Nora seemed a lot more sure of herself as soon as she was standing on two feet.

"Well, that was a waste of time," she said.

"I don't think so," said Cosmo cheerfully. "At least we know one more place that he's not!"

"There certainly are a lot of those."

"Well, let's finish up, then," he said. "We're nearly done."

We tiptoed past the dangling rope ladder and down a darkened hall. A damp wind blew toward us.

"What if someone found him already, on a lower floor?" I asked.

"They'd send up a flare and we'd see it through the windows."

"If there were any windows," added Nora.

There were three doors at the end of the hall. Cosmo hesitated.

"I don't know which way to go," he admitted. "I've never been here before."

I didn't blame him. I was so turned around myself, I wondered if we'd be able to find our way back.

Then the wooden beams groaned like a giant with indigestion. The whole house leaned to the right, and the door on the right-hand side creaked open.

I thought about what Cosmo's grandfather had said about the house taking care of them. Then I thought about the breeze that had cleared the smoke just in time for Nora to find an outlet when we were fighting the wasps.

"Try the door on the right," I said. "The house could be trying to tell us something."

Cosmo looked at me for a moment. Then he nodded and pushed the door the rest of the way open.

"Houses don't talk," stated Nora.

"You're right," I agreed. "But the Matchstick Castle isn't an ordinary house."

We had barely started walking when we came to a sudden stop. It looked like a meteorite had landed in the hallway in front of us. The ceiling was wrecked, and there was nothing above it except a few crooked beams and the stormy sky.

The floor had collapsed, too. All that was left were a few splintered boards sticking out into empty space.

Leaning out and shining our flashlights down, we could see that the hallway below was also mostly gone. It was too dark to see any farther than that.

"Unless he's a pole-vaulter, there's no way your uncle could be on the other side of *that*," said Nora.

She was probably right. But I gave a shout: "Uncle Kingsley!"

Cosmo and Nora joined in. Then we waited.

I thought I heard something. From the looks on their faces, Cosmo and Nora did, too.

"UN-CLE KINGS-LEY!" we yelled again at the top of our lungs. I held my breath and listened so hard, I thought I would sprain my ears.

"I'm in here!" said a voice at the other end of the ruined hallway.

"Uncle Kingsley?" called Cosmo.

"Cosmo? Is that you?"

"Yes! It's me! And two friends! Don't worry, we're here to rescue you."

I thought I saw Cosmo's long-lost uncle in the opposite doorway, but our headlamp beams were getting wiped out by the falling rain. How had he survived up here for a whole year?

"Is your father with you?" asked Uncle Kingsley. His voice was so weak, I could barely hear him.

"Don't worry, we'll get you out of there!" shouted Cosmo.

"And how do you propose to do that?" muttered Nora. "By flying?"

She had a point. Without a floor in front of it, the other doorway was as high up as a window in a tower.

"We'll climb across and then lower him down."

"Lower him down where?"

"To the nearest floor that hasn't collapsed. We can find our way back from there."

Cosmo took the rope off his shoulder. He tied one end around his waist and one around mine.

"Am I going with you?" I asked.

"Not yet. I want you to let the rope out carefully as I go. If I do fall, I don't want to fall all the way down."

Cosmo walked confidently out onto the biggest of the splintered floorboards. It dipped a little, making him look like a diver on a diving board—except, instead of a pool of water under him, there was only inky darkness.

I spread my legs and braced myself, holding the rope with both hands.

Cosmo started bouncing up and down.

"What are you doing?" asked Nora nervously.

Cosmo bounced higher, and higher, and, just before I heard a loud *CRACK*, he jumped into the darkness and pouring rain.

"Wait!" called Uncle Kingsley from the opposite doorway.

But Cosmo was past the point of no return. I watched the broken board tumble into the void—when I looked up, Cosmo was above us, hanging from a ceiling beam like a trapeze artist.

I let out some slack in the rope as Cosmo hoisted himself onto the beam and crawled toward the top of the broken wall.

"That's actually really smart," said Nora. "I mean, he could still break his neck, but it's the best way to get from here to there. The top of the wall is the only thing connecting the two points."

I wasn't sure how smart he was, but he was definitely brave. As we watched from the shelter of the doorway, Cosmo stood up on the crumbling wall and held his arms out like a tightrope walker. Without a roof or a ceiling to protect him, he was completely exposed to the storm. The wind made him stumble and the rain made his hair hang in front of his eyes, but he put one foot in front of the other until he was halfway to where Uncle Kingsley waited.

"He's going to make it!" breathed Nora.

I let out some more slack. It seemed like there would be just enough rope for Cosmo to get across. But if he fell, I didn't know if I could support his weight. I was just starting to look for a place to brace myself when it happened.

Lightning flashed and thunder cracked, like fireworks going off, and a big gust of wind pushed Cosmo off balance. He windmilled his arms frantically, but it was too late. He fell off the wall.

The rope went tight over the ceiling beam. I tried to dig in my heels, but they slid across the floor as I got pulled toward the edge of the bottomless hallway.

"HELP!" I yelled.

Nora reached for me and missed. I felt a sickening roller-coaster drop in my stomach as I got launched into space.

Cosmo was falling upside down ahead of me. "Whoops!" he said.

Then there was a jerk on the rope, and I swung toward the doorway where Uncle Kingsley was waiting. Because he'd fallen from the other end of the hallway, Cosmo and I were like two pendulums starting from opposite sides. At the bottom of my arc, I passed Cosmo going the other way. After swinging down, down, down, I went up, up, up—until my fingertips touched the broken floorboards by Kingsley's feet. I couldn't hold on, though, so I swung back down, almost smashing into Cosmo as he started swinging back up.

Like I learned in science class, pendulums don't swing forever. As we went back and forth, the arcs got smaller and smaller until we were barely moving at all. With the rope looped over the beam, and the two of us tied to opposite ends of the rope, I felt like one half of a pair of shoes hanging from a telephone wire. There was no way up and no way down.

CHAPTER EIGHTEEN

RESCUING THE RESCUERS

Now what?" called Nora. She and Kingsley stood in opposite doorways while Cosmo and I dangled between and below them in the hallway with the missing floor.

While lightning flashed in the stormy sky, Uncle Kingsley looked down at us like a shipwrecked sailor watching a boat sail by in the distance. I could imagine how he felt. He'd been trapped on the top floor of his own home for a whole year. He was so skinny, it looked like he'd barely had anything to eat. It was a miracle he'd even survived—and now his rescuers needed rescuing even worse than he did.

"Are you all right?" called Uncle Kingsley.

"We're fine! It's all part of the plan," answered Cosmo.

"It is?"

"Definitely."

"But how will it work?"

"It will be easier to just show you. Go ahead and get your things."

"Curious plan! But very well."

Uncle Kingsley disappeared from view.

I was just as confused as Kingsley. "Part of what plan?"

"I didn't want to worry him," Cosmo admitted. "We'll think of something."

We were still completely unprotected from the rain, and my pajamas were soaked. The rope was cutting into my waist.

"Well, we'd better think fast. Maybe Nora should go find your dad."

Cosmo shook his head, sending water flying. "Even if she can find her way downstairs, she won't know where to look for him. He's out searching, too. And if *she* gets lost, then no one will ever know where *we* are."

"Then what do we do?"

"Let's try swinging. Here, push off me."

Cosmo and I bent our knees and pressed the soles of our shoes together. Cosmo counted to three, and we pushed off, pumping our legs as if we were on swings. But sitting on a playground swing with chains to hold on to is nothing like trying to swing with a rope tied around your waist. And the worst part was that we kept smashing into each other.

After a few rounds, we had to give up. I was bruised and sore from Cosmo's elbows and knees, and I knew I'd gotten him good, too.

"We're doomed," I moaned. I'd never seen anyone get those shoes down from telephone wires.

"Cheer up! Something will happen," said Cosmo.

I didn't understand how he could always be so confident, but I wished I could be like that, too.

"Catch!" called Nora above us.

"See?" said Cosmo.

I looked up and saw Nora holding a rope with its end tied into a big knot. She took aim and then threw it overhand. She obviously didn't throw balls any more than she kicked them, but as ridiculous as she looked, she actually got the rope pretty close to us. I stretched and caught it.

"Hold on," she said and disappeared.

The rope tightened. I wound it around both hands for a better grip. Slowly and steadily, I moved toward the doorway and the splintered boards where I had fallen off. Nora was pulling me up like I was a little kid in a swing, ready for a push. I was almost to the top before I saw how she was doing it, with the rope wrapped around a wooden pillar and using her weight for leverage.

My fingers touched wood at last. I started to lift myself onto the floor at Nora's feet. Now the two of us could pull Cosmo up together.

I was so relieved, I almost wanted to hug her. "You did it, Nora! You saved us!"

Nora had a funny look on her face.

"I'm not supposed to save *you*," she said. "We're supposed to be saving Uncle Kingsley."

Then, like she had lost her mind completely, she let go of the rope and gave me a push.

"NORA!" I shrieked. "WHAT ARE YOU—"

I was already falling back down, narrowly missing a surprised Cosmo and swinging up again on the other side, when I realized what Nora had done: given me enough momentum to get all the way to Uncle Kingsley.

Twisting in midair, I saw the doorway get closer and closer. I threw myself toward it and landed flat on my stomach, then wriggled forward until I was sure I wouldn't slide backward off the broken floor. Nora and Cosmo let out a whoop behind me.

I looked up and saw a thin old man blinking in the light from my headlamp. He had long, tangled hair and a bushy beard that hung down his red velvet coat like a bib. Even though it had been decades since he posed for the picture on the back of *The Cerebral Conundrum*, he was obviously the same person. I felt like I was meeting someone who'd walked out of a history book, like Charles Darwin or Sigmund Freud or Ulysses S. Grant.

"Oh!" said Uncle Kingsley. "You're not Cosmo."

"No, I'm Brian," I said.

"Hello, Brian. I like your pajamas. I take it Cosmo's still at the end of his rope?"

"I guess so."

It was dry and a little bit quieter in the shelter of the doorway, and Uncle Kingsley and I could talk without shouting. I sat up and aimed my headlamp down at Cosmo, who grinned and waved even though the rain kept pouring down on his head. The rope connecting us was still squeezing my stomach.

"So what is the next part of the plan?" asked Uncle Kingsley eagerly.

"I'm . . . not sure. Do you have any ideas?"

"Well, just now I had an idea for a marvelous book about three daring young people who rescue grown-ups from frightening situations."

"I meant ideas for getting us back down."

Uncle Kingsley scrunched up his face and shook his head. "No. If I had, I might not have spent the last year trapped up here. All my ideas, I'm afraid, are decidedly impractical."

My heart sank like a toy car in a toilet. Even though I'd made it all the way across to Uncle Kingsley, I couldn't figure out how to get both of us back.

Uncle Kingsley was carrying a small square case in one hand and a thick stack of papers in the other. He put the papers on the floor, with the case on top so they wouldn't blow away.

He sighed. "Well, Brian, I hope you like raw pigeon eggs and moss salad, because that's about all I've had to eat for quite some time."

Just then there was a big whoosh of wind, and the whole

house leaned so far to one side that I wondered if we could just climb out a window into a tree. Then there was a tug on the rope so strong, it almost pulled me over the edge. Below me, Cosmo was pumping his legs again and swinging back and forth.

"Hold on, Brian," he called. "I have an idea!"

"Help me, Uncle Kingsley," I begged.

As the tugs on the rope got stronger and stronger, Uncle Kingsley put his arms around me and pulled. He wasn't very strong, and he smelled like my big brother Brad's gym socks—he obviously hadn't showered all year—but with both of us scrambling backward, we made it through the doorway and braced ourselves against it.

Now Cosmo was swinging like Tarzan on a vine, and it took all of Uncle Kingsley's strength and mine to hold on.

Then, just when I was sure we were going to get pulled to our dooms, the rope went slack, we heard a loud *THUMP*, and Cosmo disappeared. I took a deep breath as the rope finally stopped strangling my stomach.

"Where's he gone?" asked Uncle Kingsley, looking over the edge.

I looked, too, but I couldn't see him. From the angle of the rope, which was hanging slack but slanting down across the chasm, I guessed he must have landed on the opposite side, one floor below us.

"Well done, Cosmo!" said Uncle Kingsley to himself. "At least one of us will get back safely."

Then we heard Cosmo's voice over the never-ending storm: "My end of the rope is tied tight! Now tie off your end and slide over!"

It took me a minute to figure out what Cosmo was talking about. The rope went down steeply. If Kingsley and I followed his suggestion, we were in for a fast ride.

I shined my light across at Nora.

"It's dangerous and you'll probably be killed, but I don't think you have a choice!" she shouted.

The plaster walls near the door were disintegrating, revealing the wooden framing inside. I untied the rope from my waist and knotted it around a vertical piece of wood that looked thick and strong enough to hold our weight.

"Well, it's just like a zip line, I guess."

"Have you ever gone down a zip line before?" asked Uncle Kingsley.

"Sure," I said. I didn't want to tell him I'd been wearing a helmet and a safety harness at an amusement park at the time.

"What about my typewriter and manuscript?"

"Put the manuscript in your shirt—we'll send the typewriter down first."

Uncle Kingsley unbuttoned his shirt, held the stack of pages to his white, bony chest, and buttoned them in. If he hadn't lost so much weight, he probably wouldn't have had enough room. Then we took the belt from what Uncle

Kingsley called his "smoking jacket," looped it around the rope and the handle of the typewriter case, and knotted it.

"Here comes the typewriter!" I called, letting it go.

The box zoomed down the rope, rocking from side to side. After a few seconds, Cosmo called out that he had it.

"It's awfully steep," said Uncle Kingsley nervously.

"Which means it will be a fast trip," I said, trying to sound confident.

"Maybe you should go first?"

That would have been fine with me if I didn't have the feeling he would have been too scared to follow me down.

"Come on, we'll go together."

"If you insist," said Kingsley, sounding relieved.

I didn't bother telling him that the ride would probably be faster and more dangerous since we weighed twice as much together. Wrapping the velvet smoking jacket around the rope so we wouldn't hurt our hands, we grabbed onto the rope, with Uncle Kingsley in front.

"Ready?" I asked.

"Not entirely."

"On the count of three," I said. "One . . ."

And, before Uncle Kingsley could have second thoughts, I pushed off, sending both of us speeding down the rope.

We zoomed through the dark night and falling rain, even faster than I expected, while the rope jerked and bounced.

"I hope this is strong enough!" he shouted.

"Don't worry—it won't break!" I shouted back.

Just then, the rope broke. Nora screamed above us as we dropped like rocks.

I barely had time to realize we were falling before we landed on something soft, but it ripped and we fell again. This time we landed on something solid that collapsed with a loud *BANG*. A cloud of dust filled the air as we stopped moving.

It was pitch-dark, and Uncle Kingsley was making a weird sound, like a laughing cough, or a hyena barfing up a hair ball.

"Are you okay?" I asked.

"Ha—ha—ha—HA! MARVELOUS!" he finally choked out. "I shall have to take notes for future reference!"

My fingers were still clutching the jacket, which was tattered and torn. Dust tickled my nose and I sneezed. "Where are we?"

"In a grand old four-poster canopy bed! Can't imagine a softer landing."

My eyes focused. Through a hole in the bed's canopy, I could see one end of the rope dangling from the night sky. We must have been at least two floors below the place where we had originally spotted Uncle Kingsley.

A door flew open, and Cosmo and Nora came running in.

"Wow!" said Cosmo. "Amazing! I can't believe I didn't get to do that."

Uncle Kingsley and I climbed out of the broken bed. As I

helped him put on what was left of his jacket, the lightning flashes almost looked like party lights.

"I'm Nora," said my cousin, offering her hand to Kingsley.

Uncle Kingsley shook it. "Pleased to meet you, Nora—delighted to meet you!"

Suddenly, Cosmo started laughing, which made me laugh, and then Uncle Kingsley started laughing again, too. Even Nora couldn't help joining in. If anybody could have heard us, they would have thought we were either criminal masterminds or just plain crazy.

Then Uncle Kingsley started coughing again, and we all took turns slapping him on the back until he could talk. When he could, he had one more thing to say.

"Now, *that's* what I call a rescue!"

CHAPTER NINETEEN

UNCLE KINGSLEY'S STORY

After the rescue, we helped Uncle Kingsley climb down from the fifth floor, where we had landed, to the first floor. This time we were able to take a different route that both Kingsley and Cosmo knew well, using stairways in the front part of the house. I carried Kingsley's typewriter, Nora carried his manuscript, looking very important, and Cosmo gave him a shoulder to lean on. Sometimes we had to stop so he could rest. During one of these breaks, while Kingsley sank into an old, sagging armchair and Cosmo scouted ahead, Nora sneaked a look at the pages. I saw Kingsley watching her.

"You shouldn't read that, Nora," I said.

Nora slammed the pages shut so fast, she almost threw them down the stairs.

"I'm sorry," she told Uncle Kingsley. "I was just so curious, I couldn't help myself."

"That's quite all right," he said. "I would be very interested to know what you think about my latest work. I'm the only one who's read it so far."

"If it's even half as good as *The Cerebral Conundrum*, it's going to be amazing—that's my favorite book."

Uncle Kingsley looked as happy as a kid with two birthdays. "You've read it? You must tell me where you found your copy!"

"It was in the Boring Library."

He smiled. "Wonderful. I check it out myself twice a year in the hope they won't weed it from the collection. It seems as though my efforts have paid off! I'm so glad it was finally discovered by a like-minded reader."

Cosmo came back up the steps two at a time, not seeming even a tiny bit tired. "We should keep moving. Are you ready, Uncle Kingsley?"

He nodded, and we helped him out of the chair.

"You're a lot nicer than Nora is," I told Kingsley. "She practically bit my head off when I looked at the novel she's working on."

"So you're a novelist, too?" he asked her.

I had to give him credit: He actually sounded interested.

"Not like you," said Nora, embarrassed. "I've never

finished anything. And I hardly have anything to write about. I mean, nothing's ever happened to me."

He raised his eyebrows.

"Until tonight," she added.

"The life of an author is not easy, but if the page calls to you, you must answer—no matter where the story leads," Kingsley told her as we started to descend again. "And you're not truly a writer until you have readers. Even one can be enough. Perhaps you will permit me to return the favor and read your work?"

For a few seconds, Nora seemed to have lost the ability to speak, and her eyes shone. "I'd be honored, Mr. van Dash."

By the time we reached the first floor, the storm was nearly over. The great hall was still warm, dry, and a little hazy, even though the roaring fire had burned down to glowing ashes. Dashiell, Montague, Ivar, and Roald were slumped in chairs, looking exhausted.

The four men jumped to their feet when they saw us, pushing and shoving and trying to be the first to help their brother into a chair. Then there was another wrestling match while they took the things we kids were carrying, helped us into chairs, and gave us all tea and crackers. Personally, I think tea tastes like boiled leaves, but I let them give me a cup anyway.

Finally, Montague asked the questions we were all thinking.

"Well, Kingers, what happened? Why couldn't you get back? And how did you survive?"

Kingsley looked so tired that I half wished they would just let him rest before they pestered him—but only half. I was as curious as everybody else. And, after he drank some water and ate some crackers with sardines on them, he did seem ready to talk.

"It's quite a story," he said. "I rose one morning with a restless feeling. There was an idea rolling around in my skull, and I couldn't quite grab hold of it. I visited a few of my favorite writing spots—the library, the mushroom garden, the candlepin bowling alley—but none of them felt right. Then I had the feeling that the tale I needed to tell was a tall one, so I began climbing toward the top of the house."

"I *knew* you were searching for inspiration," said Nora.

Now that he was interested in her book, it was like she thought they had a psychic connection.

"Yes, I went all the way to the sixth floor. I even set up my typewriter and scrolled in a sheet of paper, but inspiration wouldn't come. I needed to go higher still. Did I dare climb to the seventh floor?"

"I go up there all the time," said Roald. "To keep the boat seaworthy."

"But have you *explored* the seventh floor?" asked Kingsley. "Or do you just scamper up the rope ladder?"

Roald scowled.

Kingsley turned to me and Nora. "You see, the seventh floor has been dangerously dilapidated for years. There actually used to be eighth, ninth, and tenth floors, but the tenth floor blew off in a particularly bad storm, and the eighth and ninth floors just sort of fell down on themselves."

"It was the weight of that boat that did it," muttered Ivar.

"It was your tunneling," insisted Roald. "You made the foundations unstable."

Kingsley ignored them. "Despite the danger, my story demanded that I go higher."

His eyes seemed brighter and he was looking less pale. Even his voice was getting stronger, like it was making him feel better just to tell his story.

"After carefully making my way to the seventh floor, I came to the hallway that—well, it was the hallway that you now know about," he continued. "There were barely enough floorboards to cross it, but the muse commanded that I try. And so I crept, I crawled, and lo, I made it to the other side. But, no sooner had I done so than there was a thunderous crash and the entire floor behind me fell away. My slim physique had been the straw that broke the camel's back. I was trapped!"

Rising from his chair, he started pacing in front of the fireplace.

"I was trapped in a very serviceable bedroom with, thank heavens, a bathroom *en suite*. I had a desk, a bed, and a toilet.

The toilet flushed, but the taps were dry. The only water came from the toilet!"

"You didn't *drink* it, did you?" gasped Nora.

"I did not. Thankfully, the wall outside my window was covered in clinging ivy. Each morning, I licked the dew from the leaves. I also managed to collect water by holding the lid of my typewriter case out the window during rainstorms. In winter, I melted snow in my cupped hands—I was never thirsty, you see."

"What did you eat?" I asked.

"Pigeons," said Uncle Kingsley. "And pigeon eggs. And mushrooms that sprouted from rotten boards, and dandelion leaves that I was able to cultivate from airborne spores, and moss that grew on the side of the house, and—well, that's about all. Squirrels were abundant, but they were simply too quick to catch."

"Surely you didn't eat the pigeons raw," said Montague, looking like he'd just bitten into a lemon.

"Using broken floorboards, I was able to make small cooking fires in the bathtub. But the smoke was never thick enough for signaling."

"But what about the *book*?" asked Dashiell. "Frankly, I find all this survival data uninteresting. I myself survived in Madagascar for six weeks eating nothing but ants. They were ants as big as a young boy's hand, I grant you—and delicious with pepper sauce—but we are all capable of feats of survival.

You went looking for a place in which to create your art. What I want to know is: Did you create any?"

"I did," said Kingsley proudly. "And I must confess that, as the pages piled higher, I stopped searching for ways to escape. It wasn't until I typed the words *The End* that I again crept out to the hallway to contemplate the chasm cutting me off from the embrace of my family. Alas, it was still impassable."

"Couldn't you have climbed down the ivy?" asked Ivar.

Kingsley shook his head. "By the time that thought occurred to me, I was too weak. While my fingers were quite strong from my furious typing, my arms were wasted from poor diet. But then, one day, as I was about to wring the neck of a pigeon that I had lured by mimicking the call of its mate—"

Kingsley made a cooing sound that really sounded like a pigeon, not a bearded man in a shredded velvet jacket.

"Bravo!" his brothers shouted, and we all applauded.

"Thank you," said Kingsley. "Now, it occurred to me that I might be able to train it instead. Over the next several weeks I did just that, sharing my already meager rations with the bird to encourage it on short return flights. First within the room, then down the hall and back, then finally in great circling arcs above the forest canopy. When I felt it was ready for its mission, I tied the notes to its legs and set it loose. I waited and waited for an answer. When no word came, I was dejected—that is, until I heard youthful voices above the din of the storm."

"Hear, hear," cried Montague. "Let us drink a toast to Cosmo, Nora, and Brian!"

The kids clinked teacups, and the adults drank something from a small silver flask that made Kingsley start coughing again. By then the light outside the windows had turned deep purple. The night was almost over.

"Will you attempt to publish this new work?" asked Dashiell.

"Indeed I will. I have a strong feeling the twenty-eighth try shall prove lucky and produce my second published novel. I would be happy to invest the proceeds in repairing the seventh-floor hallway. As soon as I have caught up on my correspondence, I will mail the manuscript to my agent, Mr. Seth Hamuel—I can only hope the nonagenarian still walks the streets of New York."

Montague stood up and started clearing away the cups and plates. "Perhaps you already have good news waiting on some previous project. There's quite a pile of mail. We would have tried harder to keep up with it, but we never dreamed you'd be away for so long."

"And most of it *is* for you, you know," added Roald.

I spotted William White's warning letter on a corner of the big table, still folded like a paper plane. I picked it up again.

“I hate to say this when everyone’s so happy,” I said. “But those envelopes by the door are bad news.”

They all looked at the heap of unopened mail lying next to the front door and then back at the letter in my hand.

“Are you sure you wouldn’t like something to eat first?” asked Uncle Montague. “Bad news is so much more agreeable on a full stomach.”

“We don’t have time,” said Nora, glancing anxiously out the window. “We have to get home before my parents wake up and find us missing. We got grounded the last time we came here.”

“Grounded?” repeated Cosmo. “What does that mean?”

I gave the letter to his dad. “You need to read this right away. Your home is in danger, and you only have three days to do something about it.”

I didn’t know what else to say. The thought that I might never see the Matchstick Castle again gave me a big empty feeling in my stomach.

Dashiell put both hands on my shoulders.

“Thank you,” he said, lowering his head and looking me in the eye. “We’ll read the letter. And don’t worry, Brian. We van Dashes are very resourceful!”

CHAPTER TWENTY

HELP IS OUT OF THE QUESTION

Back at 16 Sunnybright Circle, I had barely closed my eyes before Uncle Gary rang his bell to signal the start of the school day. I knew I should get up, but I was so tired I felt like my muscles were noodles and the blanket was made out of lead. I rolled over and pulled the pillow on top of my head. But the bell didn't stop clanging—in fact, it got closer. Then my door opened and the room filled with noise. I peeked out from under the pillow and saw Uncle Gary standing right next to the bed.

"Let me guess," I croaked. "I'm late for breakfast?"

He covered the bell with his hand.

"Friday is a school day, Brian. You should be at your workstation."

I sat up slowly, keeping the covers pulled up to my neck.

My pajamas were ripped and dirty, and I didn't want Uncle Gary to see them.

"I forgot to set my alarm," I told him.

"Well, I hope you didn't forget what you've learned so far this summer. We're going to test your knowledge with a Summer's Cool quiz. I'll give you ten minutes to get dressed and have a bowl of cereal—after that, I'm afraid I'm going to have to mark you tardy."

Uncle Gary turned to leave, and I rolled my eyes. My real teachers said *tardy*, too, but it's just the show-off way to say *late*. I got ready to throw off the covers and get dressed.

Then I froze as Uncle Gary stopped and looked back over his shoulder.

He stared at me and, for a few seconds, I wondered if he knew the truth. Then he told me to hurry up and left, shaking his head.

I yawned again, this time for real. I wanted to go back to sleep so badly. But instead, I got out of bed.

The quiz did not go well. Even though I felt like I knew most of the answers, the questions didn't make sense. I read them over and over, but the words rearranged themselves every time I looked. A couple of times, I realized I'd clicked the wrong thing at the exact same moment I clicked it—but it was too late to change my answer. Definitely a flaw in Uncle Gary's software.

"*Uh-oh! Let's try again!*" said Darren and Dara.

I'm sure I was imagining it—after all, their voices never changed—but even they sounded disappointed in me.

Uncle Gary saw the final score on his screen at the same time I saw it on mine. He whistled.

"Not looking good, Brian," he said. "Unless I see dramatic improvement soon, I think we might have to extend the school day."

There was a *THUNK* and I think he jumped as my head hit the plastic worktable.

"And, Nora, I'm not impressed with your score, either," he added.

That made me feel better, but only a little.

The rest of the morning passed so slowly that it seemed like a week of days crammed into one. But, finally, it was time for lunch. I stayed behind while Nora and Uncle Gary went down to the kitchen. I wanted to see if I had any messages from my dad, and I didn't want Uncle Gary reading along on his screen.

I found an e-mail from my friend Oscar, who thought most capital letters were a waste of time.

brian, summer practice is going really good. coach says he thinks we'll do great at the tournament. i know we'd do better if you were playing. sorry you aren't here & hope your summer isn't too BORING. sorry but i couldn't help it!!! oscar

Well, that was depressing.

I started a new message to my dad. At first, I was only going to explain what was happening in a general way, without giving him too many details. But once I started writing I couldn't stop. I typed and typed until my message filled the screen. I told Dad how Nora and I got lost in the woods and found the Matchstick Castle. I described the van Dashes' incredible house and the adventures we'd had there, even how we'd gotten grounded and sneaked out at night. The Matchstick Castle was doomed, I wrote, and I had no idea how anyone could save it.

Finally, when my fingers were almost too tired to type any more, I finished up with a question:

Dad, what should I do? What would YOU do?

I hit send, thinking my dad was probably hard at work and wouldn't read it for hours. And who knew when he would have time to answer me.

But, amazingly, a reply appeared in my in-box before I could log off. I opened it so fast, I almost deleted it by mistake.

Brian,

Just a quick message because it's my turn on the telescope. I don't have any easy answers, but it's always important to stand up for what you believe in—and especially your friends. It's only hard if you don't try.

And I believe in YOU.

Love,
Dad

An easy answer would have been nice, but his e-mail made me feel better, anyway. I wondered if he was trying to tell me I needed to help the van Dashes even if it meant going against Uncle Gary. Or that doing the wrong thing wasn't as bad as doing nothing at all.

I went to the kitchen and ate a sandwich in five bites, then grabbed my ball and went outside. To my surprise, Nora followed me. I passed her the ball, and even though she was about as coordinated as a giraffe playing with a beach ball, she managed to stop it and pass it back.

"What do you think the van Dashes will do?" I asked.

"Lose the letter, probably."

"No, they won't."

"They might. Their house is a mess, and they all seem very easily distracted."

I hated to admit it, but she was right. It was easy to imagine the van Dashes losing the letter. They were great at so many things, but maybe not so great at real life.

We kicked the ball a few times.

"Not that I want them to lose the letter," said Nora. "I want to save the house as much as anybody. But I don't know what any of us can do at this point. Rules are rules. At least we helped rescue Uncle Kingsley. Can you imagine what would have happened if the house had been demolished with him inside?"

"What kind of life are they going to have without their home? I can't even imagine them without it. They'd be like penguins in the desert or koalas in Antarctica. We have to help them save it somehow."

"But how?"

"I don't know," I admitted. "I know it sounds crazy, but I think we should ask your parents for help."

"I think they're afraid of the van Dashes—and they'd be terrified of the house. Why would they want to save it?"

"Because the van Dashes are nice. Maybe it would help if everyone got to know each other. We could invite them for dinner."

"I already know how my parents would respond to surprise dinner guests," said Nora. "Not. Well."

I passed the ball, and Nora kicked it hard without stopping it first, accidentally blasting me in the chest. I dropped to my knees and tried to breathe, but she had knocked the wind out of me.

"Does this mean I'm improving?" she asked.

"I'm going to ask your parents," I wheezed.

"Well, good luck," she said. "Now pass me the ball."

. . .

Dinner that night was quieter than usual. Nora and I were both so exhausted that we were practically falling asleep in our food, and it seemed like even Uncle Gary and Aunt Jenny had run out of things to say.

"How's the new hard drive running?" Aunt Jenny asked him.

"Very well," said Uncle Gary. "I'm just glad I had all the Summer's Cool files backed up."

Uncle Gary stabbed a piece of casserole with his fork. Aunt Jenny took a sip of iced tea.

"And are you ready for the Boring Art Fair next month?" asked Uncle Gary.

"Getting there," said Aunt Jenny cheerfully. "I still have to glue googly eyes on about a hundred rock critters, and I'm going to need to cut a lot more old boards down to size for Home Sweet Home signs. But thank you for asking."

I wondered if all the people who lived in Boring were actually boring or if I was just lucky enough to be related to the only ones who really were.

It was time to take action. I looked at Nora and nodded, letting her know what I was about to do. She shook her head and gave me a warning frown, but I ignored it.

When I cleared my throat, Uncle Gary and Aunt Jenny swiveled their heads toward me like security cameras.

"Is something stuck in your throat, Brian?" asked Aunt Jenny, sounding worried.

"Are you choking?" Uncle Gary asked, jumping out of his chair. "If you're choking, make the universal sign: Hold both hands to your throat so we know you can't speak."

"I'm not choking," I said, and they both sighed in relief.

Uncle Gary sat back down. I honestly think he was about to give me the Heimlich maneuver.

Then I said, "We need to help the van Dash family," and for a second I thought *they* were choking.

"Help them?" coughed Uncle Gary.

"Why?" gasped Aunt Jenny.

"Because if we don't, their house is going to be destroyed! The city says it's not safe for them to live in."

"Then it's for their own good."

"No, it's not! Their house may be a little bit dangerous, but it's also amazing, and they should have the right to live there if they want to. It's been their home for a hundred years!"

"How do you know all this, Brian?"

Now for the hard part. "Well, when we were over there, the first time—"

"The *only* time," interrupted Nora, blowing my mind by lying to her parents.

"—before we were grounded," I said, "I accidentally put something in my pocket, and it turned out to be a letter, and it accidentally opened, and I sort of accidentally read it. It was from the city, and it said that the house was going to be demolished on July eleventh. That's Monday!"

"And they didn't even know because they never open their mail," added Nora.

"Where is this letter?" asked Uncle Gary suspiciously.

"I . . . taped it up and mailed it back."

If Nora could lie to her parents for a good cause, so could I. Getting grounded again would only make it harder to help the van Dash family.

"I see. So tell me if I've gotten this right: The City of Boring has declared the home of the van Dash family unfit for habitation. It has therefore condemned the property to destruction. And you think we should help . . . how?"

"*We don't know,*" Nora and I said in unison. We sounded just like Dara and Darren. Creepy.

"Well, helping them is out of the question. If the city believes their house is a danger to them and others, then that is a legal fact and it's not our business to intervene. You simply have to take one look at the van Dashes to know they don't share Boring values—and who knows what they get up to inside that house of theirs. I've heard rumors that would curl your aunt's hair."

Aunt Jenny touched her hair like she wanted to make sure it was still short, straight, and spiky.

"But have you ever actually met them?" asked Nora.

"Have you ever even seen their house?" I asked.

"No! And once the house is gone and they have moved on, I won't have to," said Uncle Gary. "This discussion is over."

CHAPTER TWENTY-ONE

VISITORS IN THE NIGHT

That night, I dreamed I was walking through a room with a green moss carpet and rock walls covered with plants and lichen. Stone chairs and a stone coffee table sat next to an algae-filled pool with croaking frogs on lily pads. There were magazines on the coffee table, but they were all written in hieroglyphics.

I wondered where everyone else was. So I left the room and went down a hall into a gym, where specks of dust floated in bright sunshine. The gym floor was half splinters and half sawdust, so I had to walk carefully. Under the bleachers, I found a passageway that led to a huge, empty swimming pool. Double doors on the other side of the pool were labeled LOCKER ROOM. I pushed them open and found myself in a long, narrow courtyard filled with short trees where silkworms were spinning thread. Then I saw an elevator.

That's weird, I thought. *Cosmo never told me there was an elevator in the Matchstick Castle.*

I pressed the up button and stepped inside. It was completely dark after the doors closed behind me.

Then I realized I wasn't alone. There were other people in the elevator.

"Who's there?" I asked.

I heard mumbling but couldn't understand the words. Though the other passengers' bodies were crowding me, their voices seemed to come from high above.

"Who's there?" I repeated, louder.

More mumbling.

I reached out, and my hand touched a big, knobby knee. Either the other passengers were as tall as giraffes or I was as short as a monkey. I jumped up, grabbed an arm, and tried to climb the body to the head so I could put my ear closer to the mouth and hear better—but before I reached the giant's shoulder, I fell off and landed flat on my back on the soft floor of the elevator.

Then I realized I wasn't lying on the floor of an elevator in the Matchstick Castle. I was on a mattress in the basement of 16 Sunnybright Circle. But it was dark, and there really were bodies crowded all around me—and now I could hear them crystal clear.

"Shh! You'll wake him up!"

"I'm fairly certain he's awake already."

"Well, shine the light in his eyes, and we'll know for sure."

"But what if he screams?"

"He won't scream. Well, he might."

"Then pinch him."

"He'll scream for sure."

I recognized the voices. They belonged to Dashiell, Montague, Ivar, Roald, and Kingsley van Dash. But what were they doing in my room?

"I'm awake," I said.

"Aha!" said someone.

"SSH!" hissed someone else, and then it sounded like the air was being let out of lots of different-sized tires while they all shushed each other.

Then it was quiet for a few seconds.

"Brian, this is Kingsley," came a whisper. "You must get dressed at once and come with us. There isn't a moment to waste! And we need Nora, too."

"Where's Cosmo?" I asked.

"Outside, standing watch."

I turned on my bedside lamp and saw the five men standing there, blinking at me. They were dressed pretty much like they had been for the rescue mission. I didn't want to go outside in my pajamas again, so I changed into jeans and a T-shirt and picked up my sneakers.

The van Dashes followed me up the stairs, but they made so much noise with their boots and equipment that I told them to wait by the back door. Then I went up to my cousin's room.

She was lying on her back with her mouth wide open, and her snores sounded like someone trying to suck the last drops of a really thick milkshake through a straw. Even though it was the middle of the night, she was already working on some nasty morning breath. I pinched her nostrils together and started counting seconds.

I got all the way to seven before she snorted, sat up, and gasped, "I'malmostdonewithmyhomeworkIpromise!"

Then she looked at me and frowned. "What are *you* doing here?"

"Get dressed and come outside," I whispered. "The van Dashes need us."

That woke her up.

We went to the back door and put on our shoes before going outside to collect the van Dashes. Then we all went around the side of the house, making about as much noise as seven wild boars. Waiting at the curb was a car that looked like it had just driven out of a historical photograph: long and black with tall white tires and a front seat that was outside the place where everyone else sat. Cosmo was behind the wheel, smiling at us.

"Hi, Brian!"

Nora came into the yard and stopped.

"You guys have a car?"

"Why wouldn't we have a car?" asked Ivar, sounding offended. "We have a boat and a plane, after all."

"And a submarine," added Cosmo.

"A submarine that *leaks*," put in Ivar, with an accusing glance at Roald.

"That's enough!" said Dashiell. "Kids, you get in the car and we'll push. Cosmo, you steer."

"Doesn't the car run?" I asked.

"Like a top," said Uncle Montague proudly. "It's a Duesy! But it isn't as quiet as these newer cars you have nowadays. So we'll push it to the corner to avoid waking your parents."

We climbed into the front seat next to Cosmo. The car was different from any car I'd ever been in, and not only because there wasn't a roof over the driver. Behind the wooden steering wheel, the dashboard was covered with round gauges that measured everything from time and speed to direction and altitude. It was like a rocket ship crossed with a stagecoach.

"We're all very proud of the Duesenberg," said Cosmo.

"I see the driver has air-conditioning," said Nora, looking up at the stars.

The grown-ups pushed, and the car started rolling forward, its metal frame creaking and its tires rubbing on the asphalt. Cosmo steered into the middle of the street, then around a curve, and pulled up in front of a vacant lot. Then Roald got behind the wheel with Ivar next to him, while

Cosmo, Nora, and I piled in the back with Dashiell, Montague, and Kingsley.

The back of the car was luxurious compared to the front: The seats were softer, and little curtains hung in the windows.

"It's the middle of the night," said Nora. "Where are we going?"

"We're going to rescue the Matchstick Castle!" said Montague.

"How?" I asked.

"Well—" said Dashiell.

There was a huge explosion and the car rocked back and forth. Nora and I looked for something to grab on to, but the van Dashes didn't even blink. Then, while the car lurched forward, stopped, and lurched forward again, Dashiell opened a small window at the front of the cab.

"Let out the clutch *slowly*," he told Roald.

"Are there seat belts in this thing?" asked Nora nervously.

"Seat belts? Oh, heavens, no," said Montague. "I find them so confining during a journey."

The car roared away, making so much noise that I was sure Uncle Gary and Aunt Jenny would wake up, along with everyone else on the block. But Roald drove fast. With luck, they would think the noise was just thunder, or a jumbo jet.

It was crowded in back. When the car turned left, Cosmo, Nora, and I got squished against Montague, who was really big, and when the car turned right, we all squished Kingsley, who was really small. Dashiell faced us on a little fold-down seat.

"How will we rescue the Matchstick Castle?" I asked again when Roald finally found a straight road.

"We're going to fight city hall!" said Dashiell.

"Fight city hall? But how?" asked Nora.

"Well, we can thank Kingsley for this wonderful plan," said Dashiell, looking at his brother proudly and patting him on the knee. "He modestly claims he's never had a practical idea in his life, but I beg to differ. According to this bureaucrat, William 'Bill' White, our home is unsafe for human habitation—which, as we all know, is simply untrue. After all, the six men of the van Dash family, and my lovely wife, Anthea, when she's at home, live there quite happily."

"Well, your brother was trapped for a year on the top floor," Nora pointed out.

"And there are doors that open into thin air," I added.

"Yes, but has anyone *died*? I ask you."

We didn't know of anyone who had, so we shook our heads.

"And now Kingsley has a wonderful new book to show for his sojourn," continued Dashiell impatiently, punctuating his thoughts with a wagging finger. "But the point is this: We have lived there quite happily for generations without bothering a soul. Now that some pettifogging, power-hungry pencil pusher has discovered us, our house has been declared a public menace. Without so much as offering us a chance to make repairs, they're planning to bulldoze our house come Monday!"

"Well, they did send you a hundred warning letters. You just didn't open them," said Nora.

Cosmo was indignant. "They could have knocked."

"They did," I said.

The van Dashes were frowning at us.

"I'm beginning to wonder," said Montague suspiciously, "whether you aren't on the side of city hall."

"Of course we're not!" I said. "We want them to leave you alone, too."

"We're just stating the facts," added Nora.

"Well, you have your facts, and I have mine. And the fact remains that we haven't bothered anyone. Can we agree on that, at least?"

We both nodded.

"So, the plan is . . . Kingers, would you care to tell them the plan?"

Kingsley leaned forward. "My plan is quite simple. We're going to sneak into city hall in the dead of night and destroy all records that the Matchstick Castle exists: the maps, the surveys, the tax assessments, the demolition orders—all of it!"

"But won't someone remember the house? You can't erase people's memories, after all," said Nora.

"A bureaucrat like White can't operate without orders,

and if there are no orders to execute, we'll go back to living the way we like and he won't be able to do a thing about it."

"You see?" said Dashiell excitedly. "Ingenious! It can't fail!"

"But why did you bring us?" I asked.

With a scream of rubber on asphalt, the car skidded to a stop, and Montague, Kingsley, Cosmo, Nora, and I all crashed into Dashiell van Dash. The driver's window slid open.

"City hall," announced Roald. "We're here!"

CHAPTER TWENTY-TWO

FIGHTING CITY HALL

Boring City Hall was a one-story, white-brick building with a flat roof, a short lawn, and a spotlight shining on a flag that didn't have any wind to make it fly. The blinds were closed in every window, making the place look like its eyes were shut. It was the most boring building I'd ever seen. Just looking at it made me want to fall asleep—or would have, if I wasn't sitting in a car with a bunch of grown-ups who were planning a break-in.

"Drive around the back," Dashiell told Uncle Roald. "We can't be seen at the scene of the crime."

Roald put the car in gear, and with a lot of lurching and a few small explosions, we went around to the back of city hall. The parking lot was empty except for an orange pickup truck, a gray car—and a white van I recognized right away.

"That's Mr. White's van!" I said. "He used it to deliver the letters. Do you think he's here?"

"That vehicle belongs to the city, dear boy," said Uncle Montague. "I'm certain our Mr. White only drives it while he is engaged in city business. After all, he is a bureaucrat, and a bureaucrat does everything by the book. At this hour, he's certain to be in bed."

I tried to imagine what William White looked like and decided he probably looked like a giant, bald ferret. It was just a guess. If he was sleeping, he was probably dreaming about new rules and ways to enforce them.

I was glad I wasn't a bureaucrat. If I couldn't play professional soccer, I'd want to be an explorer like Dashiell van Dash—even if no one ever heard of me.

Once we were parked, the adults opened the trunk and started piling equipment on the asphalt. There were wooden crates and canvas sacks, ropes and hooks, frying pans and a camping stove. There was even a yellow canary in a little brass cage.

"I use her to check for gas underground," explained Uncle Ivar when he caught me looking. "Packed her by mistake."

"Isn't this a lot of equipment just to break into a building?" asked Nora.

The men stopped, looked at each other, and then burst out laughing like she'd just made the funniest joke of the year.

"We've been adventuring since before you were born," said Ivar.

"I think we know what we're doing, young lady," added Roald.

While Montague boiled water for tea and made sandwiches, Ivar and Roald went off to "circle the perimeter," as they put it. I watched while they sneaked around the building, testing door handles and trying to look in the windows. Kingsley made notes while Dashiell sat on a funny one-legged stool, resting his chin in his hand and looking off into the distance.

"What's your dad doing?" I asked Cosmo.

"Mentally preparing for the task ahead—he says it's the reason he's so successful at adventuring."

Ivar and Roald came back and, with their mouths full of Montague's sandwiches, explained what they planned to do.

"We're going in through the back doors," said Ivar.

"They're steel, but they're not solid steel. Our battering ram will open them right up," said Roald.

"You have a battering ram?" I asked, picturing a giant log carried by dozens of sweaty Vikings.

Cosmo looked surprised. "Obviously. Doesn't your family have one?"

Montague finished his tea, set the teacup on its saucer, and dried his lips with a napkin. He unzipped a duffel bag and took out three pieces of heavy iron pipe that fit together to make a pole, with handles on both sides, that was almost as tall as he was. While Kingsley kept making notes, the other four men carried the ram up to the back doors of city hall and took a few practice swings. If there was a louder way of sneaking into a building, I sure couldn't think of it.

"Now, then," said Dashiell. "On three. One . . . two . . ."

"STOP!" yelled Nora.

They stopped mid-swing, the weight of the battering ram almost making them all fall over.

"Could this wait?" asked Dashiell politely. "We're very nearly inside."

Nora pointed at a small white disk in the corner of the closest window. A wire came out of the disk and went into the window frame.

"There's an alarm system. If you break the glass, it sends an electronic signal to the police station."

"But we're going in through the *doors*," said Ivar, like he was explaining something to a three-year-old.

"Well, if there's an alarm system on the windows, you can be sure there's one on the doors, too. If we set off the alarm, the police will be here faster than you can say *demolition orders*."

They must have realized Nora had a point, because they put the battering ram down. I felt as disappointed as they looked. This adventure was over before it had even started.

Dashiell turned to Ivar and Roald. "What's our backup plan?"

"Yes, what's the backup plan, Roald?" demanded Ivar.

"*I* was supposed to come up with a backup plan? *You* were supposed to come up with a backup plan," said Roald angrily.

"I'll just do the washing-up and pack our things," said Montague with a sigh.

"What the deuce!" cursed Dashiell.

Looking back at the heaps of equipment by the Duesenberg, I saw the rope and had an idea. "The roof! Maybe there's a skylight or something without an alarm on it and we can get in that way."

"*That's* why we brought you youngsters along," said Dashiell, slapping me on the back so hard I started coughing. "Fresh thinking!"

Kingsley started writing faster while the other uncles moved into action. Montague put away the battering ram, Ivar found a grappling hook, and Roald tied the hook to a long coil of rope. Standing near the wall, Ivar swung the hook and threw it onto the roof of the building. He pulled the rope back slowly, trying to get the hook to catch, but every time he threw, and every time he pulled, the hook fell back to the ground with a thud.

Roald jumped out of the way and just missed getting hit on the head.

"Watch where you're throwing that!"

Montague, meanwhile, was digging through the piles of supplies. At last he straightened, holding a strange, wooden contraption.

"Try this, Ivar," he said.

It was a collapsible ladder. Montague put the pieces together so fast I could hardly see what he was doing. When it was open all the way, the ladder almost reached the roof.

"After you," said Montague.

Ivar didn't look very grateful. With the rope and grappling hook over his shoulder, wearing a big duffel bag like a backpack, he climbed the ladder like he was only doing it to be polite.

We went up after him, and soon we were all standing on the wide, flat roof of city hall. It was covered in gravel and small chimneys and vents that seemed to stick up at random. Four big, white bubbles were spaced evenly apart, making a square.

"See? Skylights!" I said.

Cosmo crossed over to the nearest one and inspected it carefully. "No alarm!"

"Which one do we want, Kingers?" asked Dashiell.

Kingsley went from skylight to skylight until he found what he was looking for. He pressed his hands and nose against the Plexiglas and hissed, "This is it!"

The rest of us looked, too. At first, I couldn't see what Kingsley was talking about. In the faint red light of an exit sign, I saw a counter, some chairs, and a filing cabinet. Then I saw a sign that read: HALL OF RECORDS. If we were really going to erase all official traces of the Matchstick Castle's existence, this would be the place to do it.

Ivar took a big crowbar and wedged it under one corner of the skylight, using Montague's knee for a fulcrum. Ivar pushed, Montague gasped, and the skylight cracked open. Everyone moved forward to help lift it. After a lot of grunting and groaning and mixed-up counts of "One, two, THREE!" and "Again!" the skylight opened like a giant clam. Cool air poured out into the warm summer night.

"Because you suggested the roof, Brian, you have earned the right to go first," said Dashiell.

"Lucky," said Cosmo enviously.

I grinned, but it felt like there were moths in my stomach. What if there was something waiting down there besides paperwork?

Ivar finally got to use his grappling hook. He wound the rope three times around the nearest chimney and then attached the hook to the rope. Then he wrapped the other end of the rope around me to make a kind of harness. If I ever joined the Boy Scouts, I was going to ace the merit badges for ropes and knots.

I stood at the edge of the skylight. The five van Dash men grabbed the rope and planted their feet. I climbed over the edge, took a breath—and pushed off.

CHAPTER TWENTY-THREE

YOU CAN'T FIGHT CITY HALL

They lowered me out of the warm, humid night, where the crickets, frogs, and cicadas were making a real racket, into the cool and quiet building. A few seconds later, I was standing on top of a counter in a big room. I jumped down from the counter and shrugged off the rope harness.

"Tug three times on the rope when you're safely down," called Dashiell.

"I'm down," I called back. "I'm standing on the floor."

"Tug three times, then!" said Nora.

I gave the rope three tugs, and they pulled it back up. The only light in the room came from the moon and a glowing red exit sign. I was behind the counter where city workers helped the people waiting in line. There were filing cabinets, computers, in- and out-boxes, and trash cans.

Nora, Cosmo, Kingsley, and Dashiell came down the

rope one at a time, followed by Ivar and his duffel bag. Montague and Roald stayed on the roof to keep a lookout and to help pull us out after we were done.

"Now, then," said Uncle Ivar, rubbing his hands together. He unzipped the duffel bag and started pulling out hammers, chisels, crowbars, lock picks, and long wooden torches. When he lit a match and picked up one of the torches, Nora stopped him.

"Wait!"

Ivar glared at her, holding the match under the business end of the torch.

"The smoke will set off the fire alarm and the sprinkler system," said Nora, pointing at the little chrome sprinkler heads sticking down from the ceiling.

"Good heavens, she's right!" said Kingsley.

Scowling, Uncle Ivar blew out the match. "I'm glad we don't have such ridiculous things at home."

"Well, if you did have safety equipment such as a fire alarm and a sprinkler system, you probably wouldn't have to break into city hall in the middle of the night," said Nora.

"Whose side are you on?" I asked.

"Ours, obviously," said Nora, exasperated. "I'm just *saying*."

"Did you bring flashlights, Ivar?" asked Dashiell.

"Of course not," he huffed. "No one's ever had a problem with torches until now. Maybe our young friends brought some flashlights?"

Nora and I shook our heads. In the rush to leave, we forgot our headlamps.

Suddenly, the room was bright as day. I squinted at Cosmo, who was standing by a long row of light switches.

"If no one's here and the blinds are drawn, we can just turn these on, right?"

No one could think of a reason not to, so after our eyes adjusted, we got to work. Dashiell divided the room into sections and assigned each of us an area to search. Ivar gave us a lot of tools we probably didn't need—I had no idea how to use a blowtorch—and we spread out. We opened drawer after drawer, but most of them were empty. And none of them held the kind of stuff we were looking for, unless we were looking for half a sandwich and a shriveled apple.

"There must be an archive!" insisted Kingsley. But the search was starting to seem hopeless.

I really wanted to help, so I kept exploring. I left the lit area and went down a hall into a big, dark room where cubicles filled the floor and offices lined one of the walls. The names on the office doors seemed to glow: VERNA TATTERSALL . . . ELDON BUNK . . . WILLIAM WHITE.

Anxious to make a big discovery by myself, I had my hand on the doorknob and was about to turn it when I heard whistling: three notes, over and over, like someone kept starting "Three Blind Mice" but couldn't remember how the rest of it went.

I looked down and saw light under the door. William

White was not home in bed, dreaming of mean things he could do to people. William White was still at the office!

I tiptoed away from the door. I had to warn everyone before they came into this part of city hall, turned on the lights, and started shouting orders at each other.

But before I could take more than ten steps, I heard something that made my blood run cold: The doorknob was turning.

I dived around the corner of one of the cubicles—actually, I fell. I landed in a push-up position and froze, holding my breath.

"Hello?"

William White's voice was smooth and a little high. It was just a normal voice, and in any other situation, there was no way it would have made my heart start to hammer.

"Hello? Is anyone there?" he said.

Quiet footsteps came toward me on the carpet. Did he know I was there?

I started crawling as quietly as I could, hoping I could make it around the next corner before the bureaucrat spotted my backside.

I heard White come around the first corner just as I turned the second one. It was quiet for a moment. "Ghosts!" he said, chuckling. He started whistling his three-note song again and the footsteps went back the way they'd come. I heard the squeak of his office chair as he sat down again.

I climbed to my feet and hurried to warn the others, hunching over to stay hidden behind the cubicles.

I had just realized that the lights were out again in the other part of the building when strong hands grabbed my ankles and dragged me into a storage closet.

"Not a word, Brian," hissed Uncle Ivar. "The bureaucrat is working late tonight."

"But how did you know?" I whispered.

"I told you, we've been adventuring since before you were born."

The wait seemed endless, even though it was probably only about fifteen minutes before we heard William White's whistle approach. Uncle Ivar stiffened, and I was sure he was going to throw the door open and attack the bureaucrat.

"Let him go, Ivar," Dashiell murmured. "Stick to the plan."

I didn't even know he was in the closet with us.

A faraway door slammed, and then there was silence. William White must have called it a night at last.

We waited a few more minutes and then turned on the light in the small closet. Ivar and Dashiell were squeezed in behind me, and Uncle Kingsley was curled up on a shelf above us.

"Where are Cosmo and Nora?" I asked as we stepped out into the hall.

A cabinet door swung open under a copier, and Cosmo wriggled out, followed by a wrinkled, blushing Nora.

Everyone was so eager to get inside William White's office that the grown-ups got bunched up and stuck in the doorway behind me. But when the lights came on, Kingsley gasped.

We all saw right away what he was looking at: On a big bulletin board behind the desk, a large map showed Boring, the river, and the van Dashes' land. The Matchstick Castle was crossed out with a big red *X*.

Dashiell went closer and examined the map, tracing lines with his finger and reading the fine print. Then he snapped his fingernail against the paper. "It seems William White has plans for our land. Demolishing our house is only phase one. Phase four involves the construction of a new subdivision called Boring View Heights."

"The monster!" Ivar growled.

"Never mind that the 'Heights' would be in a valley, and these little houses won't have much of a view," added Dashiell.

"Hey, everyone, look at this," said Cosmo, bending over the desk.

He was looking at a crude cardboard model of a ramshackle house surrounded by toy bulldozers and other construction equipment.

Uncle Kingsley knelt beside him. "He's a madman," he breathed, somehow sounding disgusted and fascinated at the same time.

I agreed with him. Who else would spend their Friday night planning to destroy someone else's home?

Uncle Ivar took action. He strode over to the bulletin board, ripped down the map with both hands, and noisily wadded it up. He dropped it in his duffel bag, then swept the cardboard Matchstick Castle and all the little toys in after it.

"That's a good start," said Dashiell. "But there must be more. Memos, work orders, correspondence—the bureaucrat's tools of trade. And we simply must find the title and deed!"

We examined every square inch of William White's office. It felt strange to be in it so soon after he left—his chair and computer were still warm. While Uncle Ivar took out drawers and turned them upside down, I went behind the desk to look at a framed picture, wondering if I would finally get a good look at the bureaucrat. But, instead of showing him, or his wife, or even his kids, the picture was of a tall dog with fluffy fur and a long, bony face. The dog looked happy, but it could have been faking.

I guess it made sense that only a dog would love him. Dogs are generous that way.

It took just a few minutes before it was obvious we wouldn't find the paperwork we were looking for.

"This is hopeless!" said Dashiell. "Kingsley, I told you this plan would never work!"

"But, Dad," said Cosmo. "You told us his plan would never fail."

Dashiell looked surprised. "I did?"

Everyone nodded, especially Kingsley.

"Sorry, Kingers," said Dashiell. They shook hands and

then hugged, slapping each other hard on the back. I had no idea brothers could apologize so fast. At home, Brad and I sometimes wrote down lists of the reasons we were mad at each other.

"Do you know what I think?" asked Nora.

"That the records are buried in a secret vault under the building?" asked Ivar.

"No. That the records are in there."

Everyone turned to see what she was pointing at.

"A computer!" said Kingsley, horrified.

"I've never used one of those," said Dashiell. "We don't have one of our own, you see."

Ivar's response was more surprising. Striding over to the computer, he raised a large pickax over his head.

"WAIT!" yelled Nora.

"NO!" I shouted.

We were too late. With a mighty swing, Ivar brought the ax's full weight down on the monitor, which split wide open. He waved away a sparkling cloud of dust and then sifted through the little pieces of plastic that had spilled out.

"There's nothing here," he said. "No information whatsoever."

Nora sighed. "Cosmo, do you want to tell them?"

"Tell them what? I've never used one of those things, either," said Cosmo.

"When records are kept electronically," I explained, "you look at them on the computer screen."

"And now it's ruined—well *done*, Ivar," said Dashiell.

"But we should be able to look at the records on any of the computers in this building," said Nora. "They're probably all connected to the same server."

"Servant?"

"Server," she repeated. "It's kind of like a master computer each of these computers can call for information."

The van Dashes all just looked at her.

"I think it's easier if you show them," I told her.

Nora led everyone out of White's office to the closest cubicle, where she turned on the computer. Everyone waited silently while it booted up. When the screen glowed to life, the van Dashes oohed and aahed.

"But we still might not be able to look at the records," she said. "They're probably protected."

"How can they be protected?" demanded Ivar. "We've broken into the building, and there's no one here to stop us from taking what we want!"

"We don't know the password."

Proving Nora's point, the computer's log-in screen appeared, requesting a username and password.

"Well, how hard can it be?" said Dashiell. "I know a little rudimentary cryptology, and Kingers here probably knows a hundred thousand words."

"We won't guess it in a million years," said Nora. "First you have to know the username, and then you have to guess the password that goes with that username."

"Let's use William White as our computer user," said Kingsley.

"Good idea!" said Cosmo.

"It's probably *w-w-h-i-t-e*," said Nora.

"Now for the password," said Dashiell. "I remember a time in Istanbul when I gained admittance to a secret society by giving the password *swordfish*. Try that!"

Hoping they might actually be on to something, I elbowed Nora out of the way, then sat down at the computer and typed it in.

USERNAME AND PASSWORD DO NOT MATCH, beeped the computer.

"Try *heliotrope*," said Kingsley. "That's a lovely word!"

Even after he told me how to spell it, that password didn't work, either.

"*Chalcedony*," offered Ivar.

The suggestions came fast and furiously, from *Australopithecus* to *Zanzibar*, but none of them worked.

Suddenly, there was a *CRACK* above us, followed by a ripping sound. We all looked up and saw Montague and Roald looking down at us through a freshly opened skylight.

"We saw the bureaucrat leave," said Montague. "Fortunately, he didn't see us. Do you need anything to eat?"

"Yes, I think so," Dashiell called back. "Looks like it's going to be a long night."

But just then, after I entered Kingsley's suggestion of *tontine*, a new error message flashed on the screen.

TOO MANY ATTEMPTS. WORKSTATION LOCKED.

"What does that mean?" asked Kingsley.

"It won't let us try anymore," I told them. "We used up all our chances."

"Blast!" shouted Ivar angrily.

"Hold the food, Monty," said Dashiell. "We're coming up after all."

Kingsley wrung his hands. "It's hopeless! I should have known we couldn't fight city hall. The Matchstick Castle is doomed . . . doomed!"

CHAPTER TWENTY-FOUR

COUNTDOWN TO DESTRUCTION

I woke up late on Saturday morning, a few hours after we were dropped off. The sun was shining brightly on my windowpane, and there was a horrible scraping sound in my head. Actually, it wasn't in my head—it was outside in the backyard. I got dressed and went outside, where Uncle Gary was holding a ladder for Aunt Jenny while she scraped away loose paint from the side of the house.

"We're painting!" said Uncle Gary. "All that talk about the dilapidated old shack in the woods made me worried that we might be next in line for demolition."

"He's joking, of course," said Aunt Jenny.

"Want to guess what color?" asked Uncle Gary.

I didn't, but I didn't have to, because he told me, anyway.

"Beige!" he said.

"Isn't it already beige?"

"Nope, Brian—that's taupe."

I went back inside. I couldn't tell the difference between beige and taupe, and I didn't care. How could he joke about someone's house getting torn down? At least it was Saturday, so we wouldn't have to do Summer's Cool.

I took some waffles out of the freezer and put them in the toaster. And because Uncle Gary and Aunt Jenny were outside, I covered them in ice cream and chocolate syrup. But having dessert for breakfast didn't taste as good as I thought it would.

All I could think about was Cosmo's family. Even though their family had built the house and lived in it practically forever, they were about to become homeless because some bureaucrat thought the house wasn't safe. And maybe it wasn't safe, but Dashiell was right: No one had gotten hurt in it, at least not too badly. Uncle Kingsley was fine, and we'd all had an amazing adventure. Instead of tearing it down, they should have made it a national monument or something.

I racked my tired brain. But the really awesome plans, like moving the Matchstick Castle somewhere else so William White couldn't find it, wouldn't work. And the more realistic plans, like getting a bunch of people to help fix up the house so William White would agree it wasn't dangerous anymore, would take too long. The wrecking crew was coming on Monday morning.

Nora came into the kitchen. "All right, let's go."

"Go where?" I asked.

But she had already left the room. I jumped up and followed her into the backyard.

"Mom? Dad?" she said. "We're going for a bike ride."

"Where to?" asked Uncle Gary suspiciously.

"The library," said Nora.

"Well, all right," he said, and before he could think of anything else to say, we ran into the garage to get our bikes.

"What good will it do to go to the library?" I asked, once we were pedaling down the street.

"The van Dashes have a library, don't they?" said Nora.

She was getting pretty good at this.

No one answered our knocks when we arrived at the Matchstick Castle a little while later, so I opened the door and shouted a hello.

There was a muffled answer.

"Did someone just say, 'We're in here'?" I asked.

"I thought I heard someone say, 'Be of good cheer,'" said Nora.

"Why would someone say that?"

"Well, with everything that's going on, I wouldn't blame them for being depressed. We could all use a little cheering up."

It did kind of sound like something the van Dashes would say.

"WHERE ARE YOU?" I yelled.

"We're in here," someone answered.

“See? I was right,” I told Nora.

The problem was we still didn’t know where *here* was. It sounded like it was coming from upstairs, so we went up the grand staircase and started opening doors. The first one opened onto a deadly drop, which I guess I should have expected, and the second one opened onto a brick wall, which also didn’t surprise me. Behind the third door, there was an art studio with easels, canvases, tubes of paint, and paintbrushes all covered in dust.

When I opened the fourth door, Nora screamed—but the two people staring at us were, well, us. There was a huge mirror just inside the door. I took a step into the room and saw a whole bunch more of me step into the room, too.

“Who has a mirror maze in their own house?”

“My brother Dash, that’s who,” said Uncle Kingsley, whose reflection suddenly appeared over Nora’s shoulder, making her shriek again. “But I also find it a useful place to meditate when I am pondering the blurry line that separates fact from fiction, and the many selves we all possess.”

“Who cleans all the glass?” she asked.

“When the dust gets thick enough, it just sort of falls off. Now come! We’ve just begun the family council. Fortunately, we can take a shortcut through here.”

Uncle Kingsley led us through the mirror maze in a series of turns I would never have been able to remember. At the end of it, he slid a mirror to one side, and we came out in a room that made Nora and me gasp.

Dark wooden blinds kept out the morning sun, but enough lamps were burning that I could still see what looked like either a museum's worth of artifacts or the world's greatest garage sale. Obviously, the stuff in the main hall was only a sneak preview of the stuff Dashiell collected on his travels: animal horns and feathered headdresses, ceremonial masks and mummified cats, wooden carvings and bronze armor—all jumbled up with maps, globes, books, and samples of insects, plants, and minerals.

In the center of the room, Dashiell, Montague, Ivar, Roald, and Cosmo were sitting around a big, round table, looking serious.

"Pull up a seat," whispered Cosmo.

I sat down next to Cosmo, feeling out of place, and Nora sat down next to Kingsley.

"The chair moves to recognize Brian Brown and Nora Brown of Sixteen Sunnybright Circle, Boring, Illinois," said Uncle Montague. "All those in favor?"

"Aye," said Dashiell, Kingsley, Ivar, Roald, and Cosmo.

"Motion carried," said Montague, banging the table with a curved ram's horn. "The purpose of this meeting is to debate a course of action on the peril currently facing the Matchstick Castle. I will begin by soliciting ideas. All formalities of the van Dash family rules of order will be observed. There will be no interruptions"—he gave Roald and Ivar a stern look—"and no comment until head of council calls for it. As a courtesy to our guests, we will first offer the floor to them. Brian, what is your plan for saving the Matchstick Castle?"

I felt like a spotlight had suddenly switched on and caught me picking my nose.

"Well . . . first I wondered if we could move it," I said, "and then I wondered if we could fix it up, but I don't think the first plan will work and I don't think there's time for the second one. From what we saw in William White's office, I don't know if there's anything that would stop him, anyway."

Montague tapped the horn on the table. "Both suggestions have already been mooted and overruled. Nora? Your ideas?"

Nora shook her head. "I'm sorry. I don't have any good ideas, either. We asked my parents if they would help us and they said no."

"I think we should sabotage their demolition equipment," said Cosmo, jumping to his feet, his eyes wild. "Pop the tires and pour sand in the engines!"

Montague banged him into silence. "Wait until you are called upon, young man."

"Sorry, Uncle Montague."

"The chair accepts your apology. Now you may begin."

Cosmo sat down. "I'm done."

"We will take your suggestions under consideration."

Then Uncle Ivar stood up.

"The chair recognizes Ivar van Dash," said Montague.

"I say we poison the bureaucrat," announced Ivar.

"Murder? Now I know you're mad!" snapped Roald.

"Not *fatally*," continued Ivar. "There is a kind of poison, brewed from the saliva of a certain kind of toad, if it eats a certain kind of mushroom, that will put a man to sleep for several years. Just like Rip van Winkle! That would buy us valuable time."

"I know that amphibian well," said Dashiell. "*Melanophryniscus droolinensis*. Indigenous people feed it the caps of the red-spotted toadstool."

"It won't help!" said Roald.

Montague banged the table. "No comment until called upon!"

Kingsley stood up, then sat down again and started paging through his notes.

Dashiell rose.

"The chair recognizes Dashiell van Dash," said Montague.

"I hope you recognize me, Monty," said Dashiell with a grin. "I'm your younger brother. Now, I think Ivar may be on the right track. But what good does it do to put a man to sleep at his desk, or in his home? What if he wakes up sooner than expected? No, I say we kidnap him—"

"You're mad! Both of you!" interrupted Roald, which made Montague bang the ram's horn even louder.

"—put him to sleep and kidnap him and take him to a remote cave where some trusted accomplices can make sure he doesn't die and doesn't wake up. I know a small island off the coast of Venezuela that would suit our purposes admirably."

"And what's to prevent them from appointing a new bureaucrat in his place?" thundered Roald. "What then? Will you poison and kidnap all of city hall?"

Before I knew it, I was standing up. I could tell from the way Nora was looking at me that she thought I had no idea what I was doing, and she was right. But poisoning and kidnapping William White seemed like such a terrible idea that I had to say something. And, anyway, couldn't they get lawyers to help them fight it in court or something? That always worked on TV.

"The chair recognizes Brian Brown," said Uncle Montague.

I cleared my throat. "Why don't you just fight it? You know—"

I didn't have a chance to finish my sentence.

"Fight?" said Roald.

"FIGHT!" said Ivar, jumping up again.

"You know, it never even occurred to me," said Dashiell.

"Oh, goody," said Cosmo.

"History has proven—" said Kingsley.

"The chair recognizes Dashiell," said Montague. "The chair also recognizes the enthusiasm in the room for this idea."

Dashiell stood slowly, shaking his head. "Here we are debating all sorts of skulduggery, and in walks a boy with a man's courage. He's right! Have the van Dashes gotten where they are today by kidnapping and poison? Of course not!"

As he continued, he began pacing the room, punctuating his speech with clenched fists and sweeping arms. "The bureaucrat is counting on our meek surrender. In his mind, the Matchstick Castle is already torn down and the van Dash estate has become Boring View Heights, a neighborhood of homes where each one is no different from the next. But come Monday morning, when the bulldozers and the wrecking ball roll up the road to the Matchstick Castle, we will meet them head-on—we will meet them and turn them back! We will look the wrecking ball in the eye and we will not blink!"

At that, the van Dashes all leaped to their feet, cheering, stomping, and pounding on the table. Cosmo actually jumped up on the table and did a war dance while Montague put his mouth to the ram's horn and blew so loud I had to plug my ears.

Nora and I looked at each other. We both knew that what the van Dashes were thinking wasn't what I meant at all.

But what they were planning sounded a lot more exciting.

CHAPTER TWENTY-FIVE

PREPARING FOR BATTLE

The rest of Saturday was a blur as we helped the van Dashes get ready. We were gone for so long that Nora made us bike over to the real library and check out books before we went home, just in case her parents got suspicious. But when we got home before dinnertime, Uncle Gary and Aunt Jenny didn't say anything. I guess they were exhausted.

Now that they'd actually started painting around the windows and doors and under the eaves, I could see there was actually a slight difference between taupe and beige. The combination of colors gave the house the look of a peeling sunburn. After dinner, Uncle Gary and Aunt Jenny went straight to bed—and a little while later, so did Nora and I. I guess we were exhausted, too.

On Sunday, the library was closed, so we said we were

going swimming and then to see a movie, or two movies if we felt like it.

"Ride carefully," said Uncle Gary.

I think he barely even heard us. He was standing in the front yard with a paintbrush in his right hand and a paint bucket in his left, looking at the house like it was his own castle to conquer.

When we were with the van Dashes, we worked hard—or at least I did. While Nora helped Kingsley carry a notepad and a pair of binoculars up to the SS *Vincible*, I helped Ivar load wooden boxes of dynamite onto a mining cart underground.

"What do we need dynamite for?" I asked him. "I thought the whole point was to avoid demolition."

Ivar grunted. "Trust me, we're not setting it off in the house. And this isn't enough to do serious damage. My supplies are so low, I'm afraid this won't be much more than a distraction to a full-frontal assault."

The crates were small but heavy. Lifting one with both hands, I stumbled on a rock and would have fallen if Ivar hadn't grabbed me before I landed on my butt.

"Careful!" he hissed. "This is old dynamite. Highly unstable. Drop it, and we won't need a detonator. We'll both go off like human cannonballs!"

"Maybe I should go help someone upstairs?" I asked, kind of hoping he would agree.

He shook his head. "We've got a job to do."

We lowered the boxes into the cart and then pushed it down the rusty rails into the darkness. Ivar lit a cigar, used it to light a lamp, and then hung the lamp on the front of the cart.

"Do you really want to put that near the dynamite?" I asked.

"I'm sorry, but I can't see in the dark," huffed Ivar.

"I could go get a couple of flashlights."

"Quit trying to run off and push the cart, Brian."

I pushed. The wheels groaned as lamplight flickered on timbers that seemed too old and frail to hold up the tons of rock above our heads.

"Is it true there's a chest of gold down here somewhere?"

"That's the family lore. If we can believe the stories, there's more than enough gold to finish the job old Angus started. There's probably enough to rebuild the Matchstick Castle with new lumber and buy every inch of land in the county, too. Wonder how a certain bureaucrat would feel about that."

We reached a junction, and Ivar paused, studying the rock above us like he was looking at the sky. Then he threw the switch, and we went down the right-hand tunnel for a while.

Then he stopped again.

"We'll leave the first box here," he said, taking a long coil of wire off his belt.

. . .

In the evening, Nora, Cosmo, and I went out into the forest with Uncle Montague. The sun was going down, the shadows were getting long, and I still wasn't sure I understood the plan.

"We're supposed to chase the wild boars?" I asked.

"What's going to keep them from chasing us?" asked Nora.

"Wild boars will chase you if they think they've got the upper hand," explained Montague. "But they also know when to retreat. They're actually quite intelligent, as is your common pig. Swine, I fear, are unfortunate victims of stereotyping."

"So how will *we* get the upper hand?" I asked.

"Well, we outnumber them. And we'll try to surprise them, too. They typically raid my garden around nightfall. By circling around in the woods and coming at the garden from downwind, we should smell them before they smell us."

He held out a hand and we slowed down.

"Would someone please creep ahead to take a look?"

"I'll do it!" said Cosmo. He ran to the edge of the clearing, stopped, dropped to all fours, and crawled out of sight.

"So we chase the wild boars into the holding pens on the other side of the garden?" asked Nora. "What if they don't want to go into the pens?"

"That is the trickiest part of the plan," admitted

Montague. "We shall have to spread out and try to funnel them in."

Even if we did catch the wild boars, I didn't see how they would help us on Monday. If we couldn't control them, they seemed just as likely to attack us as the demolition crew.

"So how are we using the boars?" I asked.

"They will introduce a crucial element of chaos," said Montague.

Swatting a gnat, I flashed back to my first encounter with a wild boar. The animals wouldn't know the difference between a kid and a construction worker—they'd probably attack everyone. "But how will that help?"

Before he could answer, we heard pounding feet and heavy breathing, and Cosmo ran out of the trees. He was panting so hard, he could barely talk.

"What is it, boy?" asked Montague.

"INCOMING!" hollered Cosmo, jumping out of the way just in time to avoid a furry gray missile that exploded out of the woods behind him.

Montague jumped right, Nora jumped left, and I jumped straight up in the air as the boar scattered us like bowling pins. Then two more boars came out of the woods, and it was like a greased pig contest at a county fair, only in reverse because the pigs were chasing the people.

"Dodge them!" shouted Cosmo.

"I'm trying," said Nora.

Uncle Montague moved a lot faster than I would have

expected for such a big guy, and he didn't look as afraid as the rest of us. I think I even heard him humming while he spun and dodged the danger.

But I wasn't sure how much longer we could avoid the sharp hooves and tusks of the boars. My legs were getting tired, and the tusks were getting closer.

"Climb the trees!" shouted Montague. That was easy for him to say. None of the trees around us had branches low enough for us kids to grab.

Montague must have realized that. Sidestepping a boar and giving it a little kick, he said, "To me!" and leaned his back against the nearest tree. Cosmo understood right away what he wanted. He ran straight at his uncle, raised his foot, and got boosted right into the branches.

"Go, Nora!" I shouted, running an extra circle to lead the boars away from her. I headed back toward the tree with all three of them right at my heels and jumped on Montague, who practically threw me up into the tree. Then the whole tree shook as Montague clambered up after me. It was hardly big enough for four people, and Uncle Montague must have weighed as much as all of us combined.

But he made it, and we held on, and even though the boars seemed mad as wasps, they couldn't reach us.

Montague looked up at me, his red face as cheerful as always.

"The only problem with chaos is that it can be a wee bit unpredictable."

. . .

We never did catch the boars, so we gave up on that part of the plan. If you ask me, it was for the best. The plan was so complicated, I could hardly remember it all, anyway—and the final piece of it involved Roald's submarine.

"If we should lose the battle and the house should fall, we'll make a strategic retreat," Roald explained. "We can navigate down the Mississippi to the Gulf of Mexico, and from there to the open sea, where we'll seek refuge on a friendly island."

"It won't come to that," insisted Dashiell.

"I think Roald's right," said Kingsley. "We should be prepared—just in case."

We had been so busy getting ready for the battle that I hadn't had time to think about the possibility that we could lose. I don't think anyone else had been thinking about that, either. But after Kingsley said *just in case*, the mood became somber.

No one said much of anything a little while later as we carried suitcases of clothes and provisions downstairs into the brick-lined tunnels and stopped at a pair of wooden doors. Ivar clicked a glowing red button, and we heard the *put-put-put* of an old motor. After a minute, the motor stopped and the red light went out.

Ivar opened the doors, and we all walked into a big wooden elevator car. They actually had an elevator, just like in my dream. It didn't go up, though.

"The Matchstick Castle was built on top of a mine, which was built on top of an extensive cave system," explained Dashiell while the elevator rattled down. "Not just on top, but in and around, all tangled up. The miners used the caves often as it saved them a lot of digging. And then someone had the bright idea of tunneling all the way to the river so they could ship the ore to the smelter by barge instead of carting it to the railroad. In later years, all this was used to transport bootleg whiskey—but that's a story for another day."

The elevator car was really just a platform with a rickety, waist-high railing. An old electric bulb showed the rough rock walls of the elevator shaft and, sometimes, tunnels and caves leading off into the darkness.

At the bottom, the elevator car stopped with a bump. Everything went dark.

"Lightbulb lasts twenty years and picks today to stop working," grumbled Ivar.

Nobody had a flashlight, a flare, a torch, or even a candle, so Ivar lit a cigar and we followed the glowing spark out of the elevator and into a cold, pitch-black tunnel that sloped downhill.

We walked and walked. It would have felt like being in outer space, except there weren't any stars. And water probably wouldn't have been dripping on my head in outer space, either.

Finally, I saw a faint light outlining two tall arched doors.

When we reached them, I realized they were at least three times as tall as I was.

We all put our shoulders against one of the doors and pushed. And pushed again. The door was so heavy, it hardly budged. But then, finally, it opened enough to let us through and we went outside, squinting and blinking at the dying sun.

A wide muddy river stretched out in front of us. Tall cliffs towered behind us. Bushes and trees lined the shore on both sides.

And, at the end of a wooden dock, water splashed against the top half of a submarine.

"How . . . ?" I asked.

"World War Two surplus," said Roald, pushing past me. "It's in perfect working order."

"It *leaks*," said Ivar.

"Perfectly normal. All old tubs leak a little. You would, too, if you were seventy-five years old."

"I'll follow you in the rowboat," Ivar growled.

Roald boarded the sub, opened the top hatch, and went inside. Ivar climbed aboard but stopped outside the hatch. Passing the bags from hand to hand, we had the submarine fully loaded in minutes.

"Can we go inside?" I asked Dashiell.

"I'm very sorry, Brian, but I'm afraid we're short on time," he said. "Another day."

I pushed a twig off the dock with my shoe and watched

it spin away in the current. What good is having friends who own a submarine if you don't even get to go inside?

Roald's head popped out of the conning tower. He scowled at Ivar. "The bow compartment is filled with rocks!"

"They're not rocks, they're *minerals*," said Ivar.

"Rocks or minerals, you've overloaded it," groused Roald, climbing down the tower and jumping onto the dock.

Ivar stepped toward him, his face flushed. "I'm not leaving my mineral collection behind for some bureaucrat to confiscate!"

"As if he's interested in that!" retorted Roald, glaring. "Besides, we've all left things we care about. I'm leaving the *Vincible*."

"You can't bring a boat on a submarine!"

"And you can't bring rocks, either!"

"Minerals!"

The two were squaring off like boxers when Montague and Dashiell stepped forward to pull them apart. It seemed like something they were used to doing. Montague wrapped Roald in a bear hug, while Dashiell put Ivar in an arm lock.

"Gentlemen, remember your manners—and remember why we're here," scolded Kingsley.

"Wait, where's the submarine?" asked Cosmo.

Only a minute before, the submarine was right next to us. Now there was only fast-moving, muddy brown water. While we all watched Roald and Ivar argue, the submarine had sunk, sending the van Dashes' food, clothes, and supplies to the bottom of the river.

"I told you it leaked," said Ivar to Roald matter-of-factly.

"It was your rocks that did it!"

"You said it wouldn't sink."

Released by Montague, Roald stalked back toward the tunnel. "Well, if you think I'm letting you on board the zeppelin after this, you're sorely mistaken!"

Dashiell followed him. "It's just as well," he said with a shrug. "I never like having a backup plan, anyway."

CHAPTER TWENTY-SIX

THE WRECKING BALL

The bulldozers came early. The wrecking ball did, too.

The next morning, Nora and I were dressed and ready a little while after the sun came up. Unfortunately, Aunt Jenny had made pancakes for breakfast. Normally, I can eat pancakes like a fireman, but this was a delay we didn't need. It seemed to take Aunt Jenny forever to make the pancakes and even longer for Uncle Gary to eat his share. And when Aunt Jenny asked him whether she should make another batch, I groaned out loud.

"Sounds like you kids are anxious to get back to Summer's Cool after that long weekend," said Uncle Gary.

I shook my head at Nora. Sometimes her dad was like a bad detective: clueless. But we still hadn't been able to think of a way to get out of the house on a Monday morning.

I decided to go bold. “Uncle Gary, Nora and I need to be excused from school today.”

From the look on his face, you’d think I told him we were going to get tattoos.

“And why is that?” he asked.

“Because they’re going to demolish the Matchstick Castle today and we’re going to help stop it!”

“Oh, no, you’re not,” said Uncle Gary. “You’re going to log on to those laptops and do your schoolwork.”

Nora looked scared of what her dad was going to say next, so I figured there was no time to lose. It was time to go even bolder.

“Yes, we are,” I said. “Nora—RUN!”

I jumped up and ran without even looking back to see if Nora was following.

“Wait!” called Aunt Jenny.

Nora was right behind me. I was actually proud of her.

My backpack was waiting in the garage where I’d left it. I hit the garage door opener and pulled on my backpack, and we rolled our bikes under the rising door before climbing on.

Uncle Gary was right behind us as we tore off down the sidewalk, his feet slapping the pavement like size-eleven pancakes. We shifted gears and pulled away.

“Sorry, Dad!” yelled Nora.

“You know what you just earned?” he yelled. “A lot more Summer’s Cool!”

Then we were on the path, pedaling all out to beat the bulldozers to the Matchstick Castle.

Branches whipped us, bugs bombed us, and spiderwebs got caught in our hair, but we didn't care. We had to get inside the house before it was surrounded. Turning from the path onto the dirt road, I skidded so hard I practically slid all the way across the road, then dragged my bike out of the way as Nora did the same thing.

I looked over my shoulder, half expecting to see a bulldozer right behind us, but there was nothing. Just a road crisscrossed by shadows in the early morning sun.

"Come on," I panted, starting to pedal again. "Almost there."

When we came out of the forest, though, we slammed on our brakes. It looked like the demolition had already started. A tall crane with a wrecking ball rolled slowly toward the Matchstick Castle on big caterpillar treads, followed by two big bulldozers, a front-end loader, and three dump trucks.

Gasping for breath, Nora looked at her watch. "It's . . . it's only seven thirty a.m. They're not . . . supposed to start . . . until eight. They're . . . cheating!"

We watched, hypnotized, as the crane pulled up in front of the house. The bulldozers revved their engines louder and louder, making blue smoke billow from their exhaust pipes—and then suddenly shut down. The construction workers climbed out of their vehicles and crowded around the back of a pickup truck.

"Come on, let's go!" I said, and we started pedaling again.

When we got closer, I could see the construction workers eating cinnamon rolls and drinking coffee.

We tried to ride past the men, but someone stepped out in front of us, forcing us to hit the brakes. It was a brick-faced, wall-sized man with hands so big they could have snapped his clipboard in half. I guessed he was the foreman.

"Stop right there, kids," he said. "This house is a public health hazard. We're about to knock it down to make sure nobody gets hurt."

"But there's a family inside," I told him.

"Oh, there's no one inside," he said. "The City of Boring delivered a hundred warning letters and never got an answer. Who wouldn't reply to a letter like that?"

"People who have more important things to do!" I said.

Then, at the exact same moment I realized we were next to a white van with tinted windows, the front door opened and a man got out.

He looked at us like we were two pieces of gum stuck to the bottom of his shoe. "Is there a problem here, Steve?"

"No problem, Mr. White," said the foreman.

The bureaucrat didn't look scary at first glance. He was average-sized and wearing black pants, a white short-sleeved shirt, and a tie that reminded me of what happens to

Chinese food when you forget about it in the fridge. His thin hair was combed straight over the top of his head, from one ear to the other. But there was something in his eyes that made me shudder—or maybe it was something that *wasn't* in his eyes.

I wanted to say something cool like, *We meet at last,* but instead, I just yelled, "You can't demolish that house! There's a family who lives in it, and they're happy, and everything would be just fine if you would go away and leave them alone. They didn't answer your letters because they didn't notice them, and I know that sounds crazy, but it's the truth!"

White shook his head. "All that is immaterial. I am responsible for enforcing a certain set of rules governing our community. Those rules exist for the health and safety of its members. If the rules are not enforced, *ergo*, our community is at risk."

"Look, there's a family inside that's definitely going to be at risk if you keep going."

"Then they'd better come out now. We're scheduled to begin."

It was no use. I might as well have been talking to a computer. I got off my bike. Nora looked puzzled, but she did, too.

"Can you hold this a second?" I asked White.

Frowning, he reached out and put a hand on my bike.

"Would you hold mine?" Nora asked Steve.

He raised his eyebrows, but he held her bike.

Now the bikes were between us and the two men, and

when we took off running toward the house, we had too much of a head start for them to catch us.

"You kids come back here!" yelled White, but we were already going up the steps of the Matchstick Castle.

The door swung open, and Cosmo and Montague pulled us inside.

"Whew!" said Cosmo. "I was starting to worry you wouldn't make it in time."

"Come in, come in—quickly now," said Montague, slamming the door behind us.

The van Dashes had been working all night, and the place looked ready for a siege. The windows were boarded up and the furniture had been piled to make barricades.

"You should join the others on the roof," said Montague. "Do you remember the way?"

"I think so," I said.

"I'll go with you," said Cosmo, and we hurried downstairs, heading for the stairways at the back of the house.

But not before I caught a glimpse of Uncle Montague climbing a stepladder by the fireplace and lifting the old shotgun out of the antlers.

This was our second trip to the ship on top of the house, and it went faster now that we knew what we were doing. It helped that a storm wasn't threatening to blow the whole thing over. Soon we were standing on the deck of the SS *Vincible* with Dashiell, Kingsley, Ivar, and Roald, looking through binoculars and telescopes at the construction workers laying siege to the house.

I watched as the foreman handed a bullhorn to White. There was a squeal of feedback, and then we could hear his voice, crackling like an old radio.

"You, in the house! You have ten minutes to vacate the premises."

Dashiell picked up an old megaphone with the words GO, TEAM painted on the side and shouted through it: "DO YOUR WORST, OLD MAN!"

The van Dashes cheered, blew raspberries, and thumbed their noses at the men below.

Then I heard another voice and looked down again.

"Nora! Brian! I order you to leave that house!" said Uncle Gary through the bullhorn.

Aunt Jenny took it from him. "Please—we don't want to see you hurt."

I lowered my binoculars. Nora looked like she didn't know what to do. I didn't blame her. If my mom was still around, I would have had a hard time disobeying her, too.

"Don't worry, they're not actually going to demolish the house with us in it," Dashiell told us.

"I hope they at least try," grumbled Ivar. "Otherwise, we've wasted the last forty-eight hours."

I didn't know who to believe. Was White just bluffing, or was he going to attack the Castle? Real-life adventures were so unpredictable. I wanted to ask Dashiell van Dash if he felt nervous, too, but I didn't want to look like a wimp in front of Nora.

I thumbed my nose at William White and Uncle Gary, even though the butterflies in my stomach made me want to barf.

"Five minutes!" White barked through the bullhorn.

We'd lost five minutes already?

Through the binoculars, I could see the workmen putting down their coffee cups, putting on their hard hats, and climbing into their big machines. Strangely, Uncle Gary and Aunt Jenny just stood there while they started the engines and revved them until the Matchstick Castle's yard was filled with roaring noise. I could feel the powerful motors shaking the deck of the SS *Vincible*.

Then we heard another engine, louder than all the rest—but this one was above us. We looked up at the sky and saw an old silver propeller plane come out of the sun. It flew closer and circled the Matchstick Castle, dipping one of its wings as if it were waving to us.

"It's Anthea!" shouted Dashiell.

"Mom!" yelled Cosmo.

We gasped and then cheered when the plane did a corkscrew dive that turned into a double loop-the-loop.

Then the plane steadied, slowed down, and came in low over the treetops.

I cringed, almost afraid to look. "It's too low! She's going to crash!"

"She must know what she's doing," said Nora.

Nora was right. As the plane crossed the yard so low it looked like it was going to land on its own shadow, the construction workers dived out of their rigs and flattened themselves on the ground. The plane climbed steeply, turned, and then buzzed the yard again, scattering everyone—I saw William White dive into the van while Uncle Gary and Aunt Jenny ran for the woods.

Anthea van Dash's plane climbed again, flashing in the sun, and we all cheered.

"You show 'em, Pansy!" bellowed Ivar.

"Pansy?" I asked.

"A pet name. It's a long story."

Just then we heard a coughing sound, and a thin line of smoke streamed out behind the plane.

"She's lost the starboard engine!" said Roald.

The plane leveled out and turned back toward us. It was so high and far away that it was just a shining silver speck against the pale blue sky.

Then there was another coughing sound and the other engine stopped. It became horribly silent above and below us. As the plane trailed smoke from both engines, I could hear the wind whistling quietly past the Matchstick Castle.

"She'll never make it to the airstrip now," moaned Kingsley.

"No problem," said Dashiell. "No problem at all. She'll just glide on down."

His words were confident, but his voice was stretched as tight as the head of a drum.

We held our breath as the plane dropped lower and lower. Its wings were level, but it was losing speed fast. It looked like Anthea was aiming to crash-land in the crowded front yard.

"There's no room," I said.

"Well, she can't put it down in the trees," said Dashiell.

"She's too low," said Cosmo, his knuckles white on the ship's railing. "Pull up, Mom, pull up!"

He was right: The plane was too low. I watched with a sick feeling as its wheels clipped the treetops. Then the tail came up, and the plane dived nose-first toward the ground.

The people in the yard scattered again as the plane somersaulted toward them. Miraculously, everyone got out of the way in time, even though one wingtip passed so close to the foreman that he could have reached out and touched it.

Dirt, rocks, and grass flew as the plane bounced end-over-end toward the trees, hurdling a bulldozer and slicing through the crumbling brick wall. Finally, it tipped over and collapsed in a cloud of dust.

"Oh, Mom," groaned Cosmo.

Ivar shook his head. "She could have at least taken out that crane."

Suddenly, we heard a sound above us like a flag snapping in the wind. We looked up and scrambled out of the way in surprise as a parachutist, wearing a flight suit and flying helmet, swung out of the sky and landed on the deck of the SS *Vincible.*

"Mom!" said Cosmo, and I could hear the joy and relief in his voice.

Anthea van Dash looked like an actress from an old film, with a smile so wide it could have filled a movie screen. But her smile turned to a worried look when a gust of wind filled her parachute and started dragging her across the deck of the *Vincible.* Cosmo grabbed her feet, and Dashiell grabbed Cosmo's feet, but now the parachute was puffed up like a sail. It was going to pull them all right off the boat!

Kingsley grabbed Dashiell's feet, but he was so skinny, he barely slowed them down.

"Jump on the 'chute!" shouted Roald.

He ran, jumped, and landed square in the middle, practically disappearing. They were all about to go over the edge. Ivar followed Roald, so I did, too. The parachute looked soft and puffy, but I landed hard on the deck and couldn't see anything except for the billowy fabric. I heard Nora thump down near me.

Finally, the sliding parachute began to slow down. We slid, smacked into the railing, and stopped.

While the rest of us stomped on air pockets, Dashiell helped Anthea unstrap her harness. Then both of them stood up, all smiles. Anthea took off her flight helmet and shook out her long red hair.

Cosmo hugged her so hard, he practically tackled her.

"Welcome back, my love," said Dashiell.

"Thank you, darling," said Anthea. "What's going on here?"

He leaned over and gave her a peck on the cheek. "Bureaucracy."

"Oh, bother," she said. "If I'd known that, I might have stayed in Borneo."

CHAPTER TWENTY-SEVEN

NEGOTIATIONS

In the front yard, the wrecking crew was regrouping. William White was back on his feet, waving his arms while he gave orders.

I was feeling like I had to barf again, but the van Dashes didn't even look worried. While Cosmo and Dashiell peppered Anthea with questions about what had happened to her during the last year, the rest of us looked over the railing of the *Vincible*, watching the scene below.

Steve the foreman put his fingers in his mouth and whistled. Then he nodded at the man driving the crane with the wrecking ball. The crane rolled even closer to the Matchstick Castle, then lowered its stabilizers with a whining sound. The huge iron wrecking ball lifted into the air while the bulldozers crawled forward like hungry animals.

"What's the plan, Dash?" asked Anthea.

"Don't you worry, my dove. We've got the bureaucrat and his minions right where we want them."

"In the front yard?"

"Just wait and see."

As if on cue, the engines powered down. There was a squeal of feedback and then William White's voice came through the bullhorn again.

"For your own safety, leave the house now!"

"I told you they were bluffing," said Dashiell, inspecting the length of his fingernails. "We have the upper hand."

"Nora and Brian," called Uncle Gary, "I am *ordering* you to come down!"

Anthea turned to us. "Perhaps you should do as they suggest."

"I'm not going anywhere," I told her, folding my arms.

Nora stepped back so she couldn't see her parents. "I'll stay, too," she said firmly.

Smiling, Dashiell picked up his megaphone and leaned over the railing. "We're quite happy here, old man, and we've got enough supplies to last all year."

"Or even longer," Ivar muttered. "We can use our tunnels to sneak out at night and reprovision."

While William White, Steve, Uncle Gary, and Aunt Jenny put their heads together and talked, I tried to imagine what it would be like to spend a year under siege in the Matchstick Castle. There would be some things I would miss, like Dad, Barry, Oscar, Diego, and soccer. And there would be others I wouldn't, like Uncle Gary, Summer's Cool, and Brad.

"Will you at least come down to negotiate? Maybe we can compromise," called White, sounding a little bit whiny even through the crackly bullhorn.

"Exactly as I predicted: He wants a parley," Dashiell told us before answering White through the megaphone. "Be there in a minute!"

"Perhaps Anthea's air strike has weakened their resolve," said Kingsley hopefully.

Dashiell hopped over the ship's railing and put one foot on the rope ladder. "It's too soon to expect their surrender, but you never know what can be accomplished at the bargaining table."

One by one, we all followed him on the long climb back down to the first floor, where Montague had abandoned the shotgun at his guard post and was propelling a long table toward the front door.

"You can't," he wheezed between pushes, "sign a treaty . . . without a table."

Dashiell, Ivar, and Roald helped him lift it, and as they carried the table through the door and down the steps, I caught a glimpse of William White and Uncle Gary looking like they'd just seen a baseball team climb out of a taxi.

"Hurry, kids," urged Kingsley. "Help with the chairs."

We all grabbed chairs, and ten minutes later, the table was set up in an open spot by the overgrown swing set—but a little too close to the bulldozers, if you asked me. Montague fussed over the arrangements, covering it with a tablecloth and setting a glass of water, a pad of paper, and a pencil at every seat.

Nora and I wanted to sit on the van Dash side of the table, but there wasn't room, so we reluctantly took our places between Aunt Jenny and Uncle Gary, who was next to William White. White seemed distracted and kept looking over the shoulder of Montague, who was sitting across from him.

"It looks like you're finally coming to your senses," he said.

Montague took a pair of reading glasses out of his pocket, slipped them on, and peered at a page of scribbled notes. "On behalf of the van Dash family, on the grounds of whose ancestral home we meet, I hereby accept your call for a parley. We propose that, while the cease-fire is in effect, the rules of the Geneva Conventions be observed, while our negotiations are guided by Robert's Rules of Order. Are these terms acceptable?"

I wondered what William White would say, but he hardly seemed to be listening. Instead, he looked at each of the van Dashes in turn, like he was doing a head count: Montague, Dashiell, Cosmo, Anthea, Kingsley, Ivar, and Roald.

"Is your entire family present?" he asked.

"It is."

The bureaucrat smiled like a big brother who just grabbed the last piece of beef jerky. He nodded at Steve, who was standing behind the van Dashes. The foreman raised his arm, and the crane's engine fired. The wrecking ball began to rise.

The van Dashes jumped to their feet, tipping over their chairs.

"It's a trick!" yelled Cosmo.

Montague shook his finger furiously at White. "You, sir, are a scoundrel! This whole thing is nothing but a plot to seize our land."

Anthea slapped her forehead. "I can't believe we fell for this," she groaned.

They turned around, ready to run back inside.

But Steve and the rest of the construction workers—about two dozen of them—had formed a human wall between the table and the Matchstick Castle.

"By the powers vested in me by the City of Boring, I order this house to be destroyed!" said White, struggling to make himself heard over the noise.

The van Dashes rushed the wall of workmen, but they were hopelessly outnumbered. They couldn't get through.

I tried to stand up and felt Uncle Gary's hand on my shoulder, pushing me down in my seat.

"Stay right here," he warned.

Next to me, Aunt Jenny had practically immobilized Nora in a terrified hug.

The wrecking ball was all the way up. A cable slowly started pulling it back. When the cable was released, it would swing forward and crash into the house with devastating force.

"Quick! What's our backup plan?" demanded Dashiell.

"You told me you don't believe in backup plans!" said Ivar.

I couldn't stand up, so I went down, slithering out of my seat. Uncle Gary grabbed but missed as I dropped to all fours under the table. I took my backpack from under my chair and scrambled out the other side, climbing over fallen chairs and sprinting toward the crane.

"Brian, stop!" shouted Uncle Gary.

"Aim for the center of the house," William White bellowed to the crane operator. "Try to knock it down in one swing!"

I unzipped my backpack, took out my soccer ball, and put it down on a little patch of grass. I was going to have to make the shot of my life.

While the crane operator pushed and pulled his levers, getting ready to swing the wrecking ball, I counted off six steps, then ran forward and kicked the ball as hard as I had ever kicked it before. It rocketed through the air, zoomed into the open window of the crane's cab, and hit the operator right on the forehead.

Soccer players use their heads all the time, but the crane operator wasn't expecting a ball to crash into his cranium. He pushed a lever when he should have pulled—or maybe it was the other way around. The crane started spinning backward, away from the Matchstick Castle, and the wrecking ball started dropping.

Everyone ducked as the crane arm kept turning and the wrecking ball looked like the world's deadliest yo-yo whirling over our heads. As it made a full circle, it crashed into a corner of the house, pulverizing a bunch of old boards. Through the hole in the wall I could see somebody's bedroom with an unmade bed and clothes hanging out of dresser drawers.

The crane operator stopped the cab, but the wrecking ball was still spinning. It had too much momentum to stop and began wrapping around the crane's stabilizers.

In the confusion, most of the van Dashes had broken free of the construction workers and were heading for the house. Ivar was wrestling with Steve while Cosmo held on to the big man's back like a monkey riding King Kong.

William White stalked toward me, his fists clenched in rage. "If that equipment is damaged, you'll have a lot to answer for!" he yelled.

"If you destroy that house, *you'll* have a lot to answer for!" I yelled back.

"Grab him," he ordered two of the construction workers.

I don't think they wanted to, but they started chasing me anyway.

"Don't you dare hurt that boy," shouted Uncle Gary, who was too far away to help.

I ran full speed toward the front door, dodging between the bulldozers and darting under the crane, right through the shadow of the wrecking ball. Then I raced up the steps of the Matchstick Castle with the construction workers right behind me.

The door swung open, and Uncle Montague stepped out with the shotgun in his arms, its barrel pointed at the sky.

"Stop right there!" he thundered.

They stopped.

"Turn around and go!"

They hesitated. Uncle Montague pulled the trigger, and the gun went off with a deafening *BANG*. The construction workers turned around and took off just as Ivar and Cosmo reached us. We all piled into the house, and Montague closed the door behind us.

I stared at the gun.

Then I stared at Nora, who had somehow gotten away from her mom and made it inside.

"Your parents are going to kill you," I said.

She grinned. "It would be pretty funny if they killed me to keep me safe."

"Was it necessary to discharge that firearm?" asked Kingsley.

"Don't worry. I'm shooting blanks," chuckled Montague. "This old thing is strictly for scaring unwanted guests. My boar-hunting rifles are safely locked up."

"Look!" called Cosmo, who was peering through a crack in a boarded-up window.

Everyone crowded around, trying to see. Finally, Roald pulled a couple of boards off so we all had a view of what was happening in the front yard.

The wrecking-ball cable had crippled the crane, which looked like a giraffe down on one knee and about to fall over. A group of men was helping the operator climb down from the cab. William White, meanwhile, looked like he was demonstrating a weird new dance. After rubbing his wispy hair with both hands, he started jumping up and down and waving his arms.

"Does the bureaucrat have ants in his pants?" wondered Anthea.

"It could be a frog," suggested Cosmo.

Then he started yelling, and we could hear him even without the bullhorn.

"Take your places, men, and commence demolition!" he ordered.

The men looked at the house. Then they looked back at him. Nobody moved.

"You heard the boss," said Steve. "Get to work."

"My daughter is in that house!" said Uncle Gary.

"And your nephew," added Aunt Jenny, "and another whole family, too."

"Then I suggest they GET OUT NOW."

William White loosened his tie and climbed onto an enormous bulldozer. Uncle Gary chased after him, but Steve, who seemed to be the only one still following White's orders, held him off with one arm, like a high schooler playing a game of try-and-hit-me with a sixth grader.

White revved the engine, ground the gears, and before we knew it, the caterpillar treads were propelling the massive machine toward the front steps of the Matchstick Castle while Uncle Gary and Aunt Jenny watched in helpless horror.

Inside, we all took a step back from the window.

"Time for your diversion, Ivar," announced Roald.

"Bit of a problem there." Ivar was behind us, turning a small metal box in his hands like it was a Rubik's Cube he couldn't solve. "And I just put a fresh battery in, too."

"That bulldozer's going to tear through this house like it's paper," said Nora, her face white with fear.

"He's just bluffing again," said Dashiell.

"With all due respect, Dash," said Kingsley, "this time, I have to disagree."

"Maybe we should slip out the back door?" said Anthea.

Outside, the bulldozer was getting even closer. It moved surprisingly fast for something that looked like it weighed twenty tons.

"Blow the dynamite!" demanded Roald.

Ivar knelt down, tugging on two long wires that snaked across the floor and disappeared under the door to the basement.

And that's when I spotted it: Right by my foot, there was a break in the cord.

The van Dashes moved halfway across the room and stopped, like they couldn't make up their minds whether to stay put or escape. When the bulldozer came through, the house was going to collapse on top of all of us—William White included.

I picked up the loose wires. "Uncle Ivar, is this what you're looking for?"

His eyes got so wide that I knew the answer. I could barely hear him over the roar of the approaching bulldozer when he said, "Twist them together!"

I connected the copper ends and felt a tingle as a charge of electricity passed through my fingers.

There was a sound like a thousand garbage trucks falling off a cliff into a parking lot. The building swayed, dust fell from the rafters, and we all bent our knees and put out our arms for balance as the floor rose and fell like a cresting wave.

"Cowabunga!" yelled Cosmo.

CHAPTER TWENTY-EIGHT

THE BATTLE OF MATCHSTICK CASTLE

The floor stopped moving. We all ran to the front door and looked out just in time to see William White's bulldozer slide into a smoking crater.

Nobody was on any of the other heavy equipment, which was lucky. While the workmen gaped at the giant hole that had suddenly appeared in front of them, there was a low rumble and a second bulldozer disappeared in a cloud of dust. Then the earth cracked open and the third bulldozer went, too. And while everyone swiveled their heads like they were at a demolition derby tennis match, the front-end loader dropped down into the ground like a trapdoor had opened beneath it.

I didn't blame them for being confused. Sometimes,

when you see something strange, it takes a little while to believe your eyes are telling the truth. But this was definitely happening.

While the ground pitched and rolled, new holes opened up, and one by one, the dump trucks disappeared.

The workmen and the drivers finally got the picture and started running up the road as fast as they could.

"What's happening?" asked Nora, who was standing behind me.

In the yard, it looked like Steve was saying the same thing using words you're not allowed to say in school.

"We're winning!" I said. "Uncle Ivar and I booby-trapped a mine shaft under the yard."

Ivar frowned. "But we only had enough dynamite for one explosion."

"Don't you see?" said Kingsley. "Once the first tunnel collapsed, it must have set off a chain reaction, making other tunnels cave in."

Once again, I wondered whether it was just a coincidence—or was the house looking after its owners?

Then there was a deep *BOOM* like an impossibly long roll of thunder, and the crane sank into the earth while the operator tried to set a new land speed record running away.

"Might have been some old dynamite down there, too," added Ivar.

Suddenly, all the van Dashes were behind us, pushing and shoving and trying to see, until we all spilled out onto the porch. The ruined yard and wrecked equipment made it look like a real battle had taken place, but it was a battle we had won. The van Dashes were cheering, and Nora and I joined right in.

Across the yard, Uncle Gary and Aunt Jenny were clinging to each other for dear life. They weren't hurt, but the dust in their hair made it look like they were wearing powdered wigs.

Then Anthea gasped, and I turned to look. William White crawled out of the crater on his hands and knees. He stood up slowly, smoke rising from his hair while dirt poured out of his shirtsleeves and pant legs. His white shirt was gray, and his ugly tie was, too. It was an improvement to the tie.

"He might be hurt!" exclaimed Montague, moving forward to help.

Anthea followed him down the steps, but White halted them with a raised hand.

"STOP RIGHT THERE," he said, his voice as cold as an outdoor pool on a winter day. Shaking with rage, he pointed a trembling finger at us.

"You have beaten me today," he said. "And you may beat me tomorrow. But you won't beat me forever. Because, in the end, city hall will always—EEAAAAAUGGH!"

His face turned bright red, and he grabbed the seat of his pants with both hands. Then he started running back and forth with choppy little steps, his tattered tie flapping behind him.

"City hall will always 'eeaaaaauggh'?" repeated Kingsley, puzzled.

"The poor man has lost his mind," said Anthea.

"Either that or he was just stung by a giant Amazonian wasp," I said. "Look!"

A swarm of huge black-and-yellow wasps was boiling up out of the ground.

"Get them away from me!" cried William White.

Thinking fast, Steve grabbed a fire extinguisher off the back of his pickup truck and sprayed a white, chemical burst at the attacking wasps. But it only slowed them down for a moment. The wasps flew up into the air, regrouped, and bee-lined toward him.

"The van!" yelled White. "Follow me!"

White bolted toward his van while Steve and his fire extinguisher brought up the rear. They slammed the doors, the engine roared, and the van fishtailed down the road with wasps trailing behind like a cloud of black smoke.

"I thought you mailed those back," I said to Cosmo.

He grinned. "I guess I forgot."

While we went out into the yard, I heard a police siren in the distance. Walking carefully to avoid the giant craters and checking to make sure no one had gotten hurt, we made our way toward Uncle Gary and Aunt Jenny.

Aunt Jenny ran to Nora and gave her a big hug. I couldn't stop her from sweeping me up in one, too.

Uncle Gary stared up at the house with an expression

that said he was sure it would fall on him any second. Dashiell walked over and stuck out his hand. "I don't believe we've met. I'm your neighbor, Dashiell van Dash, of the Illinois van Dashes."

I don't think Uncle Gary wanted to shake Dashiell's hand, but he was too polite not to.

"Gary Brown," he said. "Of the Boring Browns."

"Don't be so hard on yourself, man," said Dashiell.

"What just happened here?" asked Uncle Gary. "Were you trying to get us all killed?"

"Certainly not! As you can see, we were trying to protect our home and our family from a dangerously unbalanced municipal employee."

"If you want to talk about unbalanced, I think your whole family is as off-kilter as that tilting house of yours," said Uncle Gary, furiously rubbing the dust out of his thinning hair.

Aunt Jenny touched his arm. "Your daughter and your nephew were in that house, and Mr. White was headed right for them."

"They blew up the front yard!"

"They also saved your daughter's life."

It was very quiet as we all stood at the edge of the cratered yard, looking back at the wounded house. I could hear its old boards creaking in the gentle morning breeze. In the distance, more sirens were wailing. They were coming closer.

"Well, we'll let the police sort things out," said Uncle

Gary. "I hope they won't take long. After all, it is still a Monday, and Monday is a school day."

"Are you sure you won't stay for lunch?" said Montague.

Then there was a thudding sound as hooves pounded the ground.

"Look out!" said Cosmo. "Boars!"

"Everyone into the house!" said Dashiell. "And that means you, too, Mr. and Mrs. Brown."

Uncle Gary and Aunt Jenny turned around as three crazed wild boars burst out of the forest, heading right for us. It was hard to say what scared Uncle Gary more—being gored by a boar or going into the Matchstick Castle. But when everyone else ran toward the house, I guess he decided he didn't want to risk it alone.

He followed us up the steps, but we never made it inside. A dozen police cars came out of the trees, sirens blaring and flashers strobing, skidding to a halt wherever they could find room. That was too much for the boars. After running in a few panicked figure eights, they scattered and disappeared into the woods.

Policemen, sheriff's deputies, and highway patrolmen climbed out of their cars, looking at the wrecked yard and shaking their heads.

Uncle Gary headed straight for them, with Aunt Jenny in tow. "Thank god you're here."

Seeing all those badges made me want to run into the house, or even the woods. What if they arrested everybody and took us all to jail? But Dashiell was fearless. Right behind Uncle Gary, he strode toward them with a friendly smile on his face. Nora and I followed, a little less fearlessly.

"What seems to be the trouble, Officer?" asked Dashiell.

The nearest person in uniform took off her sunglasses, like they were somehow making it harder for her to see. She had three yellow stripes on her sleeve and a name tag that read SERGEANT COOPER.

"Looks like you'd know better than me," said Sergeant Cooper. "But we've had a report that someone was interfering with a lawfully ordered demolition, municipal property has been destroyed, and there's been illegal use of explosives and the reckless discharge of a firearm. Also that someone is harboring exotic insects."

"You forgot wild boars," added Uncle Gary.

"I see. And who is making these claims?"

She nodded at one of her men, who opened the back door of a police car. William White climbed out, followed by his faithful foreman.

"We met these two on the road, and they filled us in. We were already on our way because it sounded like World War Three was starting out here. Windows were rattling in downtown Boring."

Ivar smiled at that and nodded at me. Uncle Gary shook his head in disgust.

"I'm afraid there's been a misunderstanding," said Dashiell.

I loved the van Dashes, but sometimes they were just too polite. I pushed my way through to the front.

"Well, did William White tell you how he ordered his men to demolish the house with all of us in it? And how, when they wouldn't do it, he climbed onto a bulldozer and tried to do it himself?"

Sergeant Cooper looked at me. Then she looked at the rest of the van Dashes. Then she looked at White, who shook his head so hard I thought it would fall off. What a liar!

"Is there anyone else who can confirm this boy's story?"

The van Dashes all nodded their heads and said yes.

"Anyone who's not a part of this family?"

Nora went over to her parents and grabbed their arms. "These are my parents, Gary and Jenny Brown. They are not related to the van Dashes—they don't even like them. They live in Boring, and they want the house to be demolished, too. But they saw the whole thing!"

Uncle Gary scratched his neck and stared at the ground. "Well . . ."

"Dad, *tell them*."

Behind everyone, a cheap old car rolled to a stop, and a woman wearing a camera around her neck climbed out.

"Oh great, the media," sighed Sergeant Cooper.

"Lauren Scott, from the *Boring Update*," said the woman.

She looked more like someone's mom than a reporter, but when she started taking pictures and then whipped out a digital recorder, I was glad she had shown up.

Uncle Gary sure wasn't. With everyone staring at him, he looked like a turtle that found its shell too small to crawl back into.

"Well, it's all true," he mumbled.

"Speak up, please?" asked Lauren Scott, leaning in with her voice recorder.

Uncle Gary cleared his throat.

"It's true," he said, more loudly. "Including the part about the explosions, the gunfire, and the, um, exotic insects. But it is also true that Mr. White here ordered the demolition of the house while nine people, including three children, were still inside. And when his men wouldn't obey, he tried to do it himself."

Everyone with a badge turned and stared at William White. Sergeant Cooper folded her arms like she was waiting for an explanation and it had better be good.

The bureaucrat turned as pale as his name. His lips made an *O* like a goldfish, and I almost expected to see him blow bubbles. When he finally said something, it was in a croaking voice.

"Safe!" he said. "I was only trying to keep everyone safe. The house is a menace! It could hurt somebody. It was for their own good. And they wouldn't come out, so I had to do it. I had to knock the house down so nobody would get hurt!"

Now even the foreman edged away from William White. I saw the reporter holding her recorder up to her ear, checking to make sure she'd gotten it all.

"And what about Boring View Heights, the subdivision you wanted to build in its place?" I asked.

"Perfectly safe!" he squawked. "The whole thing was designed for normal families to live safe and normal lives. The town would double in size—there would be room for more Boring people than ever before!"

"O-*kay*," said Sergeant Cooper. "Looks like someone needs a few days off. The rest of this is above my pay grade. Is everyone here all right? Nobody's hurt?"

"That blond kid kicked me," said Steve, rubbing his shin.

"Well, my toe hurts," said Cosmo.

"And that house isn't going to fall down?"

Ivar shaded his eyes, looked the Matchstick Castle up and down, and shook his head. "Not without help, it isn't. The damage isn't structural."

"Although I do wish you'd make your bed and shut your dresser drawers, Monty," scolded Anthea. "The whole world can see your underwear!"

Uncle Montague blushed while the reporter took pictures of the messy bedroom behind the hole in the wall.

"Let's take Mr. White back to town for questioning," said Sergeant Cooper.

"Huzzah!" said Uncle Kingsley.

"Not so fast, old fella. The rest of you are coming, too."

CHAPTER TWENTY-NINE

THE END

Nora and I didn't have to go to jail, but we did get grounded again, for two whole weeks this time. And Uncle Gary gave us extra Summer's Cool, just like he promised. But neither of those things bothered me as much as I thought they would now that I knew we had saved the Matchstick Castle.

The van Dashes did spend one night in jail. The next morning, as soon as the news got out, a lawyer showed up at the police station and told them he wanted to help. A long time ago, he said, Dashiell's dad had helped his dad rescue a priceless family heirloom from jewel thieves, and he wanted to return the favor.

The lawyer said the demolition orders weren't delivered properly because they had been pushed through the mail slot instead of being handed to an actual person. I guess that's why teachers always give you report cards during class. So they didn't count, and that meant the city's attempt to destroy the house was illegal. If the lawyer was right, the city might even owe the van Dashes money—a lot of money.

"Lawyers!" sneered Uncle Montague. "Smacks of bureaucracy to me!"

"Well, until we find the gold, we'll need some money to repair the house and grounds," Uncle Kingsley reminded him.

But Nora and I learned all that later. At first, all we knew was what Uncle Gary read to us from Lauren Scott's post on the *Boring Update*. She might have been even more important than the lawyer. After someone at the *Associated Press* saw her story, all of a sudden the van Dashes were on the front pages of the *New York Times*, *USA Today*, the *Washington Post*, and even the *Boston Globe*. The first stories were just about the battle, and it seemed like most of the reporters were saying it wouldn't be fair to make the van Dashes leave their house. One of the headlines was DEATH TRAP OR BELOVED HOME? FOR THE VAN DASH FAMILY, IT'S A "CASTLE."

They started showing up on TV, too. As the reporters learned more about the van Dash family, they started sharing stories about their amazing feats: Anthea's daring flights, Dashiell's incredible discoveries, Ivar's dangerous spelunking, Roald's expert sailing, and Kingsley's heroic writing. Even Montague got mentioned for his hunting, gardening, and gourmet cooking. There were stories about the van Dash family history, one of them including an old photograph that showed Cosmo's dad and uncles when they were little kids hugging their dad after he got back from crossing the Gobi Desert with only a canteen, a flyswatter, and an umbrella.

Before we knew it, the van Dashes were famous again—really, truly famous—and everybody wanted to interview them. And suddenly, William White didn't seem so interested in knocking down their house. He probably didn't want to read another article like the one with the headline POWER-MAD BUREAUCRAT OR HEARTLESS HOME WRECKER?

Besides, he had bigger problems of his own. He was being investigated for the orders he'd given and the actions he'd taken that day. Uncle Gary told us that he would probably lose his job, and might even get charged with a crime himself.

William White accused the van Dashes of blowing up all his equipment and then stinging him with wasps, but this was hard to prove. Uncle Ivar told the police that vibrations from the machinery must have set off some old dynamite that had been left in the mines a long time ago. And the only evidence of the wasps was some big, red bumps on William White's butt.

A few days later, the Boring prosecutor announced that no charges would be filed against the van Dashes and the demolition was on hold. He was giving the van Dashes three months to submit a plan for fixing the most urgent safety issues, like installing smoke detectors and fixing the collapsed hallways, the deadly drops, the dangerous staircases, and the holes in the yard.

It was a pretty long list.

"Now," he added, "would all you reporters please go back to wherever you came from?"

Meanwhile, the Boring Historical Society contacted the van Dashes about getting the house added to the National Register of Historic Places, which would mean it could never, ever be torn down. But Anthea hated the idea.

"The next thing you know, we'll have to charge admission and give tours," she said, shaking her head in disbelief. "And they'd be expecting us to dust and tidy up!"

I wrote to my dad to tell him everything that happened, but he'd already read all about it on the Internet. Brad and Barry had, too, and now they were asking if they could come stay at Uncle Gary's too. Brad was sick of mopping floors at the pizza place, Barry was tired of getting bitten by mosquitoes, and they were both jealous of my summer adventures. And, if I ignored Uncle Gary, being grounded, and Summer's Cool—I wasn't telling them anything about Summer's Cool—it *was* an amazing summer.

Luckily for me, Uncle Gary told my brothers that hosting one nephew was enough. And where would they sleep, anyway—the garage?

He was still suspicious of the van Dashes, but I could tell that even he didn't think they were all bad.

"They put you in danger to keep you out of danger, but at least they kept you safe from that maniac, William White," he told Nora.

Even though he still thought the Matchstick Castle wasn't fit for a family to live in, after we got done being grounded, Nora and I were allowed to visit on Saturdays. But only as long as we told Uncle Gary how long we'd be gone for and promised not to go up to the seventh floor, onto the SS *Vincible*, into the mines, or inside any antique vehicles, or to fall down any deadly drops. We agreed, of course, even though we kind of accidentally broke most of the rules.

Fortunately, one of the deadly drops went straight into the little room with all the feathers, so it wasn't as deadly as it looked.

The van Dashes had mixed feelings about being a famous family again. Some days they liked the attention, and other days they wished everyone would just leave them alone. Dashiell complained that if he kept having to do interviews, he'd never have time for adventuring. They were even thinking of changing the family motto.

"We had a council to discuss it," Cosmo told me. "Dad said that since we were doing great things even when nobody was paying attention, maybe 'Do great things and let others watch' is a little out of date. Maybe it should be 'Do great things, even if no one is watching.'"

That was definitely an improvement, I thought.

Cosmo got to come over to our house, too. He loved watching TV and thought computers were so fascinating that he even liked watching us do Summer's Cool, which was weird. Kingsley also came over sometimes. He and Nora started a writing group, and they took turns reading and commenting on each other's stories. It seemed pretty boring to me, but Uncle Kingsley said lots of people were interested in his writing again and he might even be able to publish the book he wrote while he was trapped in the Matchstick Castle.

While Nora and Kingsley would yak about things like characters and setting and conflict, Cosmo and I went off on adventures in the woods. They were nothing like his dad's adventures, or even my dad's, but they were a lot of fun. We found an old sluice gate on a stream and learned how to make it go up and down. We built a fort with rocks and logs that had a food source—a blackberry bush—built in. And we made a map of all the paths through the forest. Although, by the time we were done, I knew them like the back of my hand.

I still missed my friends and my soccer team in Boston. I also missed my dad, my room, and even my brothers—a little tiny bit. But really, the only problem with my summer in Illinois was that it was going to be over way too soon.

One Saturday in late August, Cosmo, Nora, and I were kicking my soccer ball in front of the Matchstick Castle. It wasn't the best place to play because if a pass got by me, the ball would roll down the big crater William White's bulldozer had crashed into, and if the ball got past Cosmo, it would disappear into the overgrown jungle that used to be the flower beds. We had Nora standing in front of the house, so every time she missed a pass, the ball just bounced off the steps.

Cosmo was a decent soccer player. Even though he'd never played, he just seemed to pick things up quickly. Maybe that was what happened when you went to the school of life. And I was proud of Nora because she'd gotten—well, not good, but a lot less bad. Sometimes she was even the one who picked up the ball and wanted to play. She was thinking about trying out for her school team when the summer was over.

I was flying back home to Boston in a week, and I wasn't feeling too happy about it.

"So I guess nothing changes for you in September, huh?" I asked Cosmo. "We go back to school, but you just have more adventures."

"Well, I don't go to school, but I do have to learn. Mom, Dad, and my uncles always have assignments for me. Uncle Kingsley gives me books to read, Uncle Montague makes me work in the garden and the kitchen, Uncle Ivar makes me identify minerals—in a way, it's like having six teachers instead of one."

"I never thought of it that way," said Nora, kicking the ball so far to Cosmo's right that he had to dive on it like a goalkeeper to keep it from getting lost in the weeds.

Cosmo got up and kicked the ball to me. "I love them and everything, but sometimes they don't realize how much stuff everyone is giving me to do."

I trapped the ball and passed it to Nora. "I would take your family over Uncle Gary and Summer's Cool any day. No offense, Nora."

"I think I would rather have Summer's Cool than my teacher this year. Everyone says Dr. Snorkel is mean and gives tons of homework."

Cosmo was laughing so hard, he could barely pass the ball. "Did you say Dr. Snorkel?"

"She's not a medical doctor. She has a PhD and makes everyone call her *doctor*."

I was cracking up, too. I stopped the ball just before it went into the crater and passed it to Nora.

"Paging Dr. Snorkel! We have an emergency in the pool—can you unclog the drain?"

"Maybe Dr. Scuba can assist," said Cosmo, still cracking up.

Nora missed the ball, and it hit the steps. Her face got redder and redder, and then, finally, she did something I had never seen her do: She let out a belly laugh. She closed her mouth to try to stop it, but it still came out her nose.

SNORK!

SNORK! SNORK! SNORK!

Nora's laugh was so hilarious that Cosmo and I started guffawing so hard, *we* could barely breathe. And when Nora kicked the ball back to me, I watched helplessly as it rolled down into the crater and disappeared.

"I'll get it," said Cosmo, trying to catch his breath.

"No, I will," I said. "But, Nora, I think you and Dr. Snorkel are going to get along just fine."

"Take it back!" Still snorking, she ran after me. I thought of the time she chased me halfway to the Matchstick Castle. Nora and I would never be alike, but I was starting to think we could be friends, not just cousins.

I slid down the side of the crater. The ball had fallen through the hole at the bottom, so I followed, dropping onto William White's wrecked bulldozer and then waiting until my eyes got used to the darkness of the mine.

I saw a light-colored, round object a little ways away. I climbed down from the bulldozer and picked my way carefully through the rubble. Anthea had been reminding Ivar to clean up the mess in the yard, and Ivar had been promising he would, but he seemed to be better at disappearing down holes than filling them up.

As I was bending down to pick up my soccer ball, I spotted a tiny glint on the floor of the tunnel. I thought it was probably just a piece of windshield glass, but something made me reach for it.

It wasn't glass. Glass didn't break into a perfectly round shape.

"Brian, are you all right?" called Cosmo above and behind me.

Glass also wasn't gold-colored.

I brushed away the dirt and picked up a small coin, about as wide as my thumb. As I moved closer to the shaft of sunlight to get a better look, a cascade of pebbles and dirt spilled onto the bulldozer as Cosmo and Nora jumped down.

"What is it?" asked Nora.

I held the coin to the light and saw the stamped image of a woman with long hair wearing some kind of crown. I spit on the coin, rubbed it on my pants, and turned it over.

1 DOLLAR 1861 gleamed softly. The letters were encircled by some kind of wreath.

Cosmo jumped down next to me, and I held it out to him.

"It's an old gold coin," I said slowly. "Could it be . . . ?"

"It's got to be from my family's treasure," he breathed. "Where did you find it?"

I led him to the place, and he got down on his hands and knees, sifting through rocks and debris, looking for other coins. Nora and I joined him. The light was so dim that we were basically searching by touch. But after fifteen minutes, we'd had no luck.

Cosmo wasn't disappointed at all. "This coin didn't get here by itself," he said excitedly. "Uncle Ivar will find the rest of them if he has to dig up what's left of the yard to do it. And with all that gold, we won't have any problem fixing up the house. We'll repair Mom's plane and raise the submarine, too!"

Have you ever felt so happy and relieved that you didn't know what to say and the feelings all filled you up until you could have almost barfed with joy?

That's how I felt.

I handed Cosmo the coin, but he gave it right back.

"Keep it. It will be a good souvenir of your summer. Or sell if it you want—you definitely deserve a reward."

As I rubbed the small worn disc between my fingers, I felt the metal getting warmer. It felt nice and soft in a way that quarters and dimes never did. I guessed it was worth a lot of money, but I knew right then that I would never sell it. The gold coin was just like the Matchstick Castle—it was proof you could find amazing things in places you never expected.

"Give me the ball, Brian," said Nora. "Let's go tell the grown-ups."

I picked up the ball and handed it to her. Then, after putting the coin deep in my pocket, I followed her and Cosmo up into the bright sunshine of Boring, Illinois.

ACKNOWLEDGMENTS

Writing this book has been its own adventure and has required a lot of help along the way. I offer my grateful thanks to Josh Getzler and Danielle Burby, as well as Jen Besser, Shauna Rossano, and Katherine Perkins, for believing in this book and helping it see the light of day.

With her gift for specific, plot-changing suggestions, Ilene Cooper deserves special mention. Kirstin Scott reminded me to add a fart joke, among other great advice, and Ian Chipman told me to make the wasps bigger. Linda Joffe Hull knew all along that the beginning would have to move faster—and she was right. Lauren Wohl provided advice and encouragement.

Cosmo Graff, Felix Graff, Wilhelmina Graff, and Liza Hull all gave this book early reads, and their responses helped me.

Early versions were improved by the insight of Ken Wright and his team, and also by Katherine Jacobs.

I'm thankful for the support of Bill Ott and my amazing, talented colleagues at *Booklist*.

Most of all, I am indebted to my wife, Marya, and my sons, Cosmo and Felix, for their patience and understanding during the countless hours when I must close my door. Having time to write makes me a happy man and, I hope, a better husband and father.